When a writer passes, his words remain; this book is dedicated to each and every one of you that continue to read Jay's words and keep his legacy alive.

--Jenny Wilburn

Madness Heart Press
2006 Idlewilde Run Dr.
Austin, Texas 78744

First Edition
www.madnessheart.press
isbn: 978-1-955745-47-5

Beautiful

DARKNESS

JAY WILBURN

A Madness Heart Press Publication

FOREWORD

This book is important. I met Jay at KillerCon 2019. I was there because a story in an anthology I had published was nominated for a Splatterpunk Award. Jay was there because a story HE had written, "Seersucker Motherfucker," had been nominated. We shared a wall, his table and mine at the back of the vendor room of a con that I had never been to before. Jay was quiet, kind, thoughtful, and he spent a lot of the weekend watching my wife knit little hats. I didn't really interact with him much at that con. It wasn't until he blew away the competition during the Gross Out Contest that I realized what a goddamn genius he was.

He went up there, this quiet guy I had barely spoken to during the con, and exploded with energy, telling the story of his catheter extraction so vividly that I almost felt like someone was drawing a line of rubber tubing out of my shredded penis. And it was hysterical; I was crying from laughing so hard. I followed him on social media that minute.

A few months later, the pandemic crushing all of us under its weight, I invited Jay onto a 24-hour stream I was doing to kill some time. We talked for four hours. We had the sort of easy camaraderie that you expect from old friends. And honestly, I am nothing special. Jay had that energy with everyone he met. He was able to be himself and accept you for whoever you were.

We spoke regularly, and whenever I got the chance, I found myself accepting or even soliciting books from Jay. Because he was amazing, as a writer, as a friend, and he could always, seemingly without effort, make me laugh just as hard as he did that night during the Gross Out Contest. He originally dedicated this book to his wife, who saved him, who gave him strength and two children (one of them amazing, he never said which one). If you check *Room 138*, you'll see he dedicated that to Jenny too. *Curse of the Ratman* he dedicated to me, because he said it was too filthy to be dedicated to someone decent.

Why do I say all of this when all you want to do is read a book? Because I want you to understand that while Jay could write some incredibly dark things, he has always been a beacon of loving kindness to myself and every other member of the Horror community. I want you to picture that kindness while you read this book. I want you to understand that if you ever met Jay, he loved you, and not with the sort of affable, self-smug "I love everyone" bullshit you see regularly, but earnest, actually-cares-about-you love.

Jay passed away in late 2022, leaving a gaping and ever-raw wound in the community and in our individual psyches. It is an incredible honor that Jenny, his wife, allowed me to bring this collection, previously only available on Jay's website, to a wider audience . This book is important because without it, I would never have gotten to meet and know Jay, and I hope through his writing, you can relive your friendship with him or get to know him for the first time.

John Baltisberger
Publishing Editor,
Madness Heart Press

Jay Wilburn

HOTLINE

My kidneys are failing. It's a long, slow process—like falling to your death through molasses or some shit. In fact, I just came from an appointment before I got here.

I used to be an economics teacher. You remember economics? You ever meet any economists? Ever run into a group of them at a bar? Join them for drinks and then the night got real crazy? No? That's because they are imaginary, like unicorns or successful writers.

High school kids give even less of a shit about economic theory than you do. The day I threw up and passed out in class, that's what they remember. I'm on medical leave now.

Hold on. I need to take this. "Hello? ... That's me. ... Yeah, that sounds terrible. You should do that."

Okay, as I was saying, my insurance got rejected. *At first.* The best facility in my state—my region. Three months they held my referral, then let me know my insurance was out of network. Out of network? I can see the place from the window of my classroom where I threw up and passed out during the most memorable day of economics ever.

So, I had to go to a facility over in North Carolina. Not the best either. The fifth best in the state—out of five. I wouldn't bet on the fifth best North Carolina basketball team, but I'm betting my life on this place.

Since I left my job, I got that super poor person insurance. It only covers transplants in the fifth best place in North Carolina, but it is cheap as hell, so I guess I should thank all you working stiffs for subsidizing my premiums. Thanks.

Hold on … I got another … "Hey. Right … That is a tough break. … Shit, I'd kill myself if that happened to me. … That's what I said. … You're damn right."

Okay, so what I was saying is, if you're going to do something stupid, please, do it in North Carolina. Surfing on top of your buddy's car. Jumping off a balcony into a hotel pool. Drag racing. Picking up hitchhikers for sex. Do it all in North Carolina.

You can skid along a road until your face is gone, and those surgeons will divide up your guts like you are freakin' Kobe beef. They'll take your dead parts and rebuild my ass like damn Frankenstein's monster.

I got a good blood type too, so I should be a match with one of you assholes out there. You never know who will be "the one," so I got to cast a pretty wide net.

Oh, damn it. Hold on … "What? … Your parents, huh? … Yeah, that is some shit. … What are you thinking about doing then? … No shit? That's a new one. I think that'll really show them they should be sorry. Good plan, kid."

Okay, so I got all this extra time on my hands. I need to be more proactive, need to seize my destiny, you know? There are a ton of people in line ahead of me, and I need to clear them out of the queue one way or the other.

I have to drive into damn North Carolina for all my medical anyway, so I volunteer at the hotline here. Kill a bunch of birds with one *phone*, you know?

Hold on … Busy night … "Yeah, this is the hotline. …

That's the one. I assume you called for a reason. Don't leave me in suspense, baby. Lay it on me. ... Yeah, I hear you. I'd be planning to kill myself too. ... I know, but it's the truth, sweetie. ... I'm just saying, let's keep our options open. Don't take anything off the table just yet. ... Tell me what you're planning to do to yourself. ... Wait. Baby, you live in North Carolina, right? ... Perfect. ..."

I'm going to let you all go. I need to take this call.

CABIN IN THE COTTON

The boy had on no shoes as he tracked between the rows. He rolled up the cuffs of his overalls to nearly his knees but still managed to muck the inside denim.

The cotton turned stringy and dark on the plants to both sides of his path, dragging the ground in the breeze where no one bothered to pick it. The boy didn't like how the stuff felt on his ankles as he followed the curve of the rows across the field. Now that no one would pick it for free, the old man in the cabin was apt to leave the back acres to ruin in the rain, even if the market price soured just a little. It wasn't worth the nickels to him to keep it from waste.

The boy clutched the scrap of paper down by his side as the cabin with the sagging roof rose into view. Patch boards over the sides peeled away from paper and tar, baring exposed nails like angry spines. Story was the cabin had been fine and impressive at one time, but the years had not been kind to the man or the house. Only a promise from a generation past kept anyone from knocking it down for good. The land was worth more than the promise, some said, but people kept it anyway.

The note had things about the boy's mother. He mentioned his fears in it. He saved lines for everyone he knew was sick. The boy confessed wrongs as best he could remember—honest to a fault about his faults. He closed with a few lines complimenting the old man. It was the way his mother taught him to write such things.

The other boys, closer into town and farther from the bank of the river, said the old man couldn't read. He had no eyes to see and wouldn't care what folks wrote in their notes even if he did. His mother said the old man in the cabin read every word of every note even if we didn't see him doing it, so the boy was as inclined as not to believe it was so.

He left the short rows near the edge of the tall grass around the cabin and the gnarled trees that shaded the leaky roof. He wanted to roll down his pants again against the itch of the untended weeds, but the ground was still wet, so he refrained.

The boy rounded on the front door, which faced the two-lane running between town and points west. A warped post stood without the mailbox on its head. Boys who could drive liked to take bats to such things, and no one kept up with the old man's business enough to notice or replace it. The empty post seemed to match well enough with the rest of the property.

The boy wished to knock on account of custom, but he couldn't find a solid surface on the place he trusted. The screens folded away from rusted staples around the slat frame of the door. The boy reached through and unhooked the latch himself. The only part of the house determined to hold firm appeared to be the hinges, and the boy forced a gap wide enough to slip inside.

He did not wipe his feet but kept watch on the floor for nails and glass.

A figure passed from the hallway into the kitchen area.

The boy could smell it. The old man had lost his

outhouse long before his mailbox. There was a hole in the floorboards in one of the rooms. A bucket formed a semi-permanent seat, and business gathered below the planks for roaches and rats to deal with.

The boy crept forward, not wanting to surprise the old man, even though he had been by a few times before.

He sat at the table. His shirt was threadbare, and his arms under rolled sleeves looked hard and dry like leather. Even the hair over his arms was grey now. His callused hands folded on the formica in front of him. The straps on his overalls were starting to tear at the clasps but still held on as the old man let them hang loose around his hips.

The old man's head was big, especially around the forehead. His lips drooped on one side. Some folks said he had a stroke or a palsy. Others, mostly the other boys, said he was feeble in the head all along. Born dull right out of his mother, if a man that old could have ever had one. The boy often feared the old man in the cabin might be mad or dangerous below his quiet surface. How could he not be, living in a place like this?

He didn't look up or acknowledge the boy, but the boy set his note upon the corner of the table and slid it toward the old man's place, stopping just shy of the clasped fingers. The boy's approach lost its courage, and he left the folded paper there. As he withdrew his hand from the old man's table, the note popped open an inch on its last hard fold.

The old man didn't reach for it, if he saw it, and he didn't raise his gaze. He mumbled something still and small. The old man was known to talk that way, but the boy always expected something louder and deeper, the way the old man was said to have spoken in the past, when people picked the cotton for free.

The boy couldn't make out the words but knew he had heard something. It was some proclamation from the man of the house.

The boy wasn't sure if it was what the old man in the cabin wanted or if it would earn any of the things scratched on the folded paper, but he took up the broom and began sweeping. Starting with the kitchen around the old man's feet, he then moved room to room. Couldn't say he exactly thought sweeping bought a boy forgiveness for the things he listed on his paper, but he wanted to believe he did it for grace and because he loved the old man in the cabin, but who really knew? He swept anyway because there was a broom and there was always a mess.

He returned to the kitchen after spilling the gathered dust down the same hole covered by the bucket seat. Even in the darkness under the house, he saw stuff moving. In the kitchen, he found the chair and table empty. The old man was gone and so was the note.

The boy propped the broom in the corner and walked to the front room to stare at the old man's back. There he stood, facing the window with his arms crossed and the overall straps still hanging down loose around his bony hips instead of his bony shoulders.

The glass was dirty and gave a thin, shady look to the road—and the world—down both ends of the highway. The boy suspected the window had once been clean and might be again if someone did anything about it. Folks could see clearly out it then. He imagined it fell into the same tired neglect as mailboxes and leaky roofs.

"Is that it for now?" The boy didn't like how his voice sounded to his ears inside this place. The wet walls seemed to eat the sound instead of letting it bounce back naturally.

He liked it less that he couldn't hear the old man in the cabin respond at all.

He didn't know if the old man had taken the note, didn't know if it was read or ever would be. It was delivered and out of the boy's hands either way, so he forced his way out the door and past the stubborn hinges.

He crossed the weeds and reentered the curved rows between the cotton plants, which were beyond picking, beyond saving through harvest.

He kept his back to the cabin in the cotton and traveled through the field to leave the back acres of the old man's land behind. Where people wouldn't pick for free.

Story was the old man still read the notes and still gave consideration to the things in them. Word was he did the work which needed doing before the boy or even his parents were born. No one alive had seen it, but story was these things boys wrote in notes were the kind of thing the old man in the cabin forgave still.

The boy couldn't prove any of it, but he still brought his notes and still swept the floor, not knowing if the old man even cared about such things. The note was gone, and the boy decided to leave the things he had written in it for the old man in the cabin to do with as he would or wouldn't. His mother believed it and so then he believed it too.

He hated the dead, wet cotton around his ankles, and the boy thought someone should have picked it long before it got this way back when it was still bright for the harvest.

LINKS IN THE CHAIN; BOARDS UPON THE BACK

The furnace threw sparks as it flared between orange and white heat. He hammered more links into his chain and poured water over them to darken the metal, steam filling the roof of his cave. It would be easier without the chain, but breaking it wasn't an option—only adding to it. The damned thing was so heavy already and ached his old muscles, but he had to drag it out farther each day.

He set down the hammer next to the anvil and opened his fingers, hearing the knuckles crack three times each. He hauled the sack onto his back and passed the boards over his shoulder and into it one at a time. The wood was no longer fresh and straight. He used gnarled logs and driftwood pitted deep with holes. New trees were extinct from the landscape around his cave and mountain, so he was reduced to scavenging from dead and abandoned things.

He scooped the nails into the pouch on one hip, set the carpenter's hammer into the loop on the other, and then he was off. Every other step was a haul, dragging the full weight of his chain down the face of the mountain behind him.

At the bottom, he reached the beginning of the road. Few stones remained, and the edges were lost and worn invisible. The oldest crosses lined both sides, with rotting meat and ragged clothes hanging from rusted nails and spikes. He could still smell them, but the odor was weak. The stench would grow in the miles ahead, as did the number of bodies spread out farther and farther from both sides of the road.

He passed mile after mile of death until bodies, still bleeding from fresh wounds and crying from new, raw pain, begged him at both shoulders. His head ached from the noise, and his scalp burned from the sun overhead. The heat on his bald skin went from bright red to white blisters as the day wore on and the screams grew.

The crosses gave way to countryside, houses, and cities. Between them were battlefields and blight. He lifted the suffering bodies from the ground and hammered his gnarled wood into crossbeams, then used the same nails to spike them up and lift them up into crucifixion. They screamed anew and cursed him. They railed about broken promises. They cried about injustice before begging for mercy and salvation. Men confessed. Women bargained. Children stammered in confusion and asked for God.

He moved on.

He pulled a teen from the passenger's seat and nailed her mangled body onto a driftwood cross beside the street next to the missed stop sign. Her bashed skull lolled on her neck, and she stayed quiet as a result, but he knew she would scream at him tomorrow.

He dragged a boy out of the backseat. The young man had bled out a lot, but he still fought and kicked against the man on the chain. It took an effort, but he lifted the boy up on a cross next to his sister. The boy started screaming and yelled out at his sister next to wake up. The man on the chain left the mother unconscious behind the wheel. He left the drunk man sleeping in the other truck as well. They would realize what was lost when they both woke up later.

The man on the chain dragged the full weight of the links farther down the road as his pack of boards grew lighter on his back.

He lifted a man off the table of an operating room. The doctors and nurses all clawed at the dead man's flesh to try and hold on, but the man on the chain was stronger. He crucified the lost patient on the curb outside the hospital, naked, with his chest still open and ribs separated.

He took bodies from more accidents. He lifted up the oldest people away from their families. Then reunited them with more family members on the side of the road, all on crosses of their own. He took those who took themselves with guns still in their hands, pills piled in their bellies, or ropes around their necks. Even when they lifted themselves up, the man on the chain had to nail them up a few feet higher.

Then he saw her again. He had reached for her when she was a child, reached for her twice more as she grew older, and nearly brushed her flesh both times. Now here she was again. Her hair was fallen out, and her flesh clung to her brittle bones. Poisons pumped through her veins, trying to kill a bundle of cells lumped together in her scarred chest. Her breath came shallow, and life was pain for her, but still she gripped the arms of her chair until her knuckles faded from arthritic red to white.

It was finally the moment when she would be his, with him forever on the side of his road. He would look up at her each time he passed, day after day, and would think about all the times she slipped away from him. Did he admire her from all the years of pursuing her?

Hell, he might even have loved her by this point.

He reached again, but the chain pulled up short. This couldn't be happening again. He lunged forward, but the chain pulled taut, and his fingertips drew short of reaching her once more.

His joints ached, his back throbbed, and his muscles quaked from the day's work, but he turned his lips up into a smile. Even in her haggard state, she had outpaced him one more time. She limped just out of his reach before she rested again. He still had boards on his back and nails in his pouch, but he was out of links in his chain for today.

He would return to the cave and forge a few more for tomorrow. He would need many more boards too.

The man on the chain watched her for a few moments longer, so close to him but just out of his grasp. He listened to her breathe. He watched her scarred chest rise and fall with a sense of wonder. Her purple eyelids remained closed. Sometimes she opened them and saw him. Today, she paid him no respect and gave him none of her attention. She rested herself for tomorrow's journey.

He turned away and left behind the soft music of her breathing for the angry cries of the ones lifted up on both sides of his road. They shivered with the growing darkness of night and the endless pain of eternity, but they never stopped shouting out at him as he gathered his chain and returned to his cave with the full weight of the links.

He fired up his furnace and melted more metal in its white-hot belly. Lifting his heavy hammer, he added to the links in his chain and thought about her. He wondered how she felt, walking on aching bones with no chain to drag, and he felt jealous. His thoughts dwelt upon the day he would reach her, lift her up, and hold her forever. Pale lips drew into a smile as he hammered more links and poured more water. Steam filled the roof of his cave.

The new links grew dark, cold, and ready. He stacked more boards onto his back one by one by one, remembering the music of her shallow breath.

LOST AND DRAWN

He did not remember who he was after he died and opened his eyes, not in the same way living people remember things. There was enough left in mind and muscle for him to stand, so he did. He could not walk well where his skin was torn and his muscles chewed through, but the others stepped back from him, allowing him to begin his slow pace.

He had been holding someone's hand before. His fingers still clasped and released on empty air. The muscles and dull impulses still fired off from the desperate fight and struggle to hold on as they had sunk into death together. He did not remember her. There was not enough left of her to stand, so he walked alone. Still, his hand opened and closed over and over in an echo of his last act in life of trying to hold on even as the others took them apart.

Gunshots echoed through the city. Sirens and the crackle of fires burned out of control. Some of the others were drawn to these noises, sights, and temperatures. Sometimes he followed them as well. This didn't draw him as strongly as the others, so he returned to wandering quicker than they did.

At some point, cityscapes became suburbs and suburbs became country. This pattern repeated a few times, but it did not register in what remained of his mind. Occasionally, he pushed against the glass of car windows or houses. With the others, he beat on doors for a while. He walked through campsites, open RVs, or farmhouses, but he always walked out again. He crossed grassy fields and hills, getting hung in barbed wire for a while until his clothing and skin tore free, and then he walked again. His feet found road once more, and he would follow those trails for a while. Sometimes paved and sometimes dirt, but always onward.

They would be on one—one that was still living and still screaming—and pile around until there was nothing to see. Blood oozed red out along the road, and red was the only color he could see. It made him moan and growl like the others. It made the hunger, which was always there, somehow grow more desperate and sharp within him, but he walked around, he walked past, and he walked away.

The rain washed into his wounds and over his dry, pale eyes. Nothing healed. The lightning did not make him blink and the thunder did not make him flinch. The noise did not draw him. He no longer responded to gunshots or screams like the others.

Snow tripped him up and made the road hard to follow. He broke the skin of his chin down to the bone on something buried just under the snow. He did not dig for it, and there was nothing red left in him to mark the snow where he fell. He stood because he still could, and he walked. Somewhere along the road, he had finally lost his shoes. He left bare footprints in the snow as he weaved between the trees, searching for something.

He stopped at the ruins of the barn and the half-burned farmhouse. There had been many others like it, but he stared at this one. He had no way of knowing why or for how long, but he had been circling this property for some time. He had followed many of the same roads, through cold and heat, until he stumbled upon the road which led here.

He did not go into what remained of the house but walked nearer to it.

It was the tree that drew him. He lifted a hand to touch the carving in the bark on the side, down low where a child would reach. That hand still opened and closed over and over and over. He stared down at his moving fingers for some time, then used the other hand to run his fingertips over the texture of the bark and the curves in the carving.

He did not know why it mattered or why it drew him, but it did.

The stones on the hill drew him next.

They were crooked, old, and moss grew over carved letters he could no longer read anyway. Hands broke the ground from below and fought to push free. Many were more bone than flesh.

He lumbered forward and dug at the earth. He tore through grass and roots, clawed away dirt and clay with the same fervor the others tore into flesh. There was no red to see, but he saw it anyway. Both his hands opened and closed over and over as they broke into the ground. First, the nails tore free, and then the flesh split and peeled. Soon, his boney fingers matched theirs.

Heads and shoulders broke the surface. He took hold and would not let go until they were out. Some still had hair. Few still had eyes. Some were held together only by decay itself, but they could stand, so they did.

He stood with his abused hands down by his sides. Both hands were motionless for the first time since he had died.

He turned back toward the road, and the others followed because they could. He walked the road, but he wasn't alone.

NEIGHBORHOOD BUSINESS

Gabby Wilks is a bitch. She is a bitch in the morning, a bitch in the evening, and a bitch the livelong day in between. I assume she is a bitch when she sleeps too. Even the way she says my name—Roxie Stump—as if it's something dirty in her mouth. Bitch. She was a bitch before our husbands died, she was a bitch when the neighborhood threw us 70th birthday parties, she was a bitch before the zombies showed up, and she is the biggest bitch still alive on God's bloody, undead Earth.

I'd be willing to cut her a break about being such a bitch since we're all about to die if it wasn't for what she did last Saturday.

We were hiding in our separate houses next door to each other and eating the bad groceries in the back of the pantry. The ones you think you'll never get to until there's an apocalypse. The wax beans and the canned cabbage you don't even remember buying.

I hear a thump on my aluminum siding. I think … zombie—Damned Zombies!—but it keeps happening. Then, there's a thump on the gutter—like hailstone but only one. I go to the window on Gabby's side, and she's throwing pebbles from her garden against my house. Crack. One hits the window, and she acts like she doesn't even notice me spying on her.

The zombies all leave her yard and crowd around my house. She slips out with a shoulder bag like she's on a stroll. I think she's cutting loose, but she comes back about an hour later with the bag loaded down with cans from one of the other houses. I'm so mad that she left those zombies around my house and led more back to join them, but mostly I'm mad I didn't think of it first.

On Sunday, I'm tired of wax beans. I go to the dead freezer and hold my breath as I pull out the rotten hamburger I couldn't figure out how to cook before it turned. I pull back the plastic, and it's as black and dead as the zombies. I put on my gloves and then throw it out my window by the handfuls. I didn't think I could reach Gabby's yard at my age, but I was motivated. I hit her garden, I plopped her lawn furniture, and I stuck it to the side of her house. I was having so much fun I almost forget to sneak out to get cans. I shouldn't have done it, but I walked behind her back fence and dumped the rest of the hamburger on the other side of her house so she'd get zombies all around. I found some proper vegetables and canned meat over at the Haebberman's. I heard thumping in the back bedroom, and I knew it wasn't hailstones, so I got out of there. My back hurt carrying all the cans back.

The best part, Gabby sees me going back into my own house. Totally worth it.

Monday, she left her house, and all the zombies followed her. She looked like she was about to get caught, so I watched. She led them through my backyard so that they trampled all my bushes. My gardener is dead! I can't fix that mess! Once she got around the side, she broke into a sprint like she was twenty years old and not as fat as a whale. She got back into her house and lost them, so they stayed in my yard. Well played, Gabby. Well played.

Tuesday, I found my husband's portable CD player and some batteries. I started an Ann Coulter book on CD and threw it in her yard. Bingo. Zombie lawn party! I just wish I had remembered to put it on repeat.

Wednesday, she somehow caught a squirrel and trapped it in one of those hamster balls. She rolled it into my yard, and it kept bumping between my trees for an hour trying to climb. By the time the zombies tore it open, my house was surrounded. Gabby went out with her handbag again. I'd say she couldn't have eaten all those cans, but she is a BIG woman.

Thursday, I got a tetherball string on a spike from the hall closet. I nearly got bitten trying to pull this off. I stuck the spike down into her garden and led them through the yard. I gave the ball a swat and wrapped up one dead girl's neck. I then doubled back and got the zombies to tie themselves to the side of her house.

Friday, she got the zombies to eat cherry bombs and then led them past my house so they exploded guts all over my windows and siding.

I could still smell it when I started yelling out of my window with the bullhorn at her house today. She found a tuba and started blowing it back at me with her endless supply of hot air. Well, we carried on until every zombie from three neighborhoods were gathered around.

They crashed through the sliding glass doors first. Then they were pouring in from everywhere. I forgot about Gabby and hauled ass out through the mud room. They were all around me. Close enough to touch me! My heart is not ready for this sort of excitement.

As I was hobbling up the street on my bad knee just ahead of them, Gabby started waddling right beside me. Of course, she's got breath to spare to talk about what a bad person I am and how this is somehow my fault.

The zombies were gaining on us. They're dead and slow, but I'm almost seventy-one and haven't had air conditioning for weeks.

Gabby cut to the right and squeezed behind the wheel of Mr. Haebberman's Cadillac run up on the curb against his brick mailbox. I knew they'd catch me if I kept going, but I did consider it seriously. I hopped into the passenger's seat next to Gabby Wilks, and we power locked the doors just in time.

So, here I am, stuck in a car with Gabby, surrounded by zombies as I write this on Wendy's napkins from out of the glovebox. I tried to number the corners so you can follow this story in order.

I convinced her to stay silent so I could write this, and told her I was coming up with a plan. Gabby Wilks … silent … a miracle in the Age of Zombies.

I have a plan all right. I'm going to stick these napkins in the plastic sleeve for Mr. Haebberman's insurance card so no blood or zombie shit gets on my story. Then, I'm going to smile and flip up the power locks with whatever juice is left in the battery. After that, I'm going to use both legs to kick Gabby Wilks's fat bitch ass out the door. Maybe they'll get full eating that 200 pounds of rotten hamburger she carries around on her thighs.

Even if I don't survive, at least I got her last!

All right, Gabby, it's show time!!!

OUTSIDE THE CITY WHERE WE EXCRUCIATE

Easter service left me empty by sunrise, and we were still not done.

The new flowered dresses no longer held up the illusion of being anything but salvaged fabric. Colors faded.

The cross outside the church made from rotten fence posts shed dirt through the chicken wire wrapped around it. In the days before, we used to bring flowers from Spring gardens to decorate the thing in the brightest colors imaginable. Pinks, blues, and purples so obscene the blooms were difficult to stare at directly. I'm not sure I remember what makes purple different from blue now.

Our gardens are behind sheet metal fences and barbed wire. We grow shriveled blue muscadines and thin, hairy squash with pale flowers. Still, we bring the colorless squash flowers and weeds to decorate the chicken wire cross because it is Easter. We bring in the hard, hairy vegetables to keep the vermin or the neighbors from stealing it.

It tastes bitter and burns my stomach without filling it. There are extra trips out to the latrine behind the wire. I don't complain because my father watches from Heaven and my uncle is my mother's new boyfriend and he will not have it.

We file out of the church, which is the same shape and temperature as the smoke box we use for curing the small game we trap. I remember Easter used to be surprisingly cold each year. Spring would start back when I still remembered purple. Then the cold returned as we put on clothes for service meant for warmer weather. We shivered through. It does not get cold, and we do not have many surprises anymore.

The road is dusty between the church and the hill outside of town. There are empty houses between. Most of the siding and much of the wood has been scavenged, but there is enough left to imagine a town with more people where these houses were still needed.

We pass under the lookouts in the nests perched above what we have decided is the edge of our territory. It's near the shell of a gas station, and they use the posts from the old rain cover above where the pumps used to be to support the firing nests. It's far, and I don't like walking past them. It feels like we are fighting hard to defend a lot of empty space between where we really live and here.

My father used to say, "If you give up ground, they'll take that and come for the rest too."

My father died on lookout and now watches from Heaven.

The men on lookout have their hoods up and their goggles on. Their long guns lay across their laps, and they don't bother looking down at us as we pass. I want to believe it is because they are being watchful like my father used to be. I slept better in the house when he was alive and keeping our perimeter. I think, though, that they are bored with the passing of everyone in their Easter finery. Or they see where we are going and it holds their attention.

I wish I had my goggles and gear, but it is Easter, so we wear this, and we are not done.

The sun is barely up, and it is already hot.

He screams.

I want to stand farther back because I don't want him to recognize me. We were friends, sort of. It's a small town, and everyone knows everyone. The scapegoats sometimes confess in their agony and incriminate others. It can impact the next selection even a year later, or sometimes sooner if it is a bad season and another intercession is needed. There are not many good seasons anymore.

We have to line up in the order we arrive, and my family ends up near the front middle. It is a small town and getting smaller, so there are not many bad views left on Easter.

They hammer the spikes through wrists and ankles, up high on the bone, close to where his limbs are tied. I hear bone splinter even over the screams. He arches his back like a man possessed as he lays upon his cross on the ground. There is too much slack in his ropes. He'll be able to lift to breathe. He's going to take a long time to die, and it's already hot. I don't like his screams, but the ceramic spikes are in, so I hope his broken legs make this quicker for all of us.

They lift him up and position him over the pre-dug pit slot. He flaps against the wood like a flag and moans. We all brace ourselves for what we know is coming. The post drops in with a bass note thump, and the man shudders on his spikes from the impact. We all exhale at once with a whoosh.

He begins to mutter and thrash. Some of the syllables sound like words. I brace myself again for him to start naming names. My family is front and center, if he can still see.

He lifts to take a breath, and bones crackle. We can see the bulge in his legs from the breaks, but he still heaves up for air. This is going to take a long time.

He screams. "I can't take it. Just shoot me. Shoot me in the head. I'll still die. I'll still bleed. I can't suffer enough to heal the town. Just end it. I'm sorry for everything. Everything everyone ever did. I'm sorry."

He may be naming names, but it's all slurs. No one acts like they recognize any of it, so we all wait for it to be over.

I can tell it is close to midday because I'm hungry and my head feels like it's on fire without a cap. It's Easter, so we cannot wear them, and I know my scalp will be blistered tonight.

"Remember this! Remember it. Remember me. When you eat and drink and starve and nothing has changed, remember."

The flesh around the breaks is splotched green and yellow. There is a darker color building below the skin. It is difficult to make myself look at the bruises directly, but if I stare at the darkness long enough, I start to remember what purple looks like.

He goes slack and stops lifting. I don't quite let myself hope that it's over. One of the men stabs him with a shank on the end of a pool cleaning net. The body shifts, but that could have been from jostling. The blood runs down his ribs, hip, and limp genitals, flowing dark and thick. With blood like that, he may still be alive, but no one wants to wait it out.

"It's finished."

We follow the trail toward town, and my legs are watery. My body wants to collapse, but I don't want to be out here anymore.

No part of me believes the squash will be good for my stomach or the water clean after the Easter offering. There are not many surprises anymore, but another day is done, and the sun will go down again. Then it will be cooler for a little while, and maybe my father in Heaven won't be able to see as well what we have done.

WHAT SHE SAID

Dick Brewer ran for the warehouse, not because it was the best idea but because the zombies were too close for him to come up with a better option. He didn't bother to look back for his friends. Either they were with him or they weren't.

He saw blacked-out windows across the front. They were ground level but not broken out like the rest of the city. "What She Said" hung stenciled across the front of the building. It was either the name of the warehouse or a joke. Then he spotted an open door and decided that this represented his salvation, or his final mistake.

Dick hit the rough stone of the wall at the entrance as he charged into the darkness of the gap. With both hands on the edge of the door, he gave his friends a three count to get their asses inside or to be left to get their insides eaten out. Johnson's feet flew out from under him as he tumbled into the warehouse, but he kept spinning his shoes anyway like some cartoon rabbit. Willy was old, but the horde of zombies gave him the motivation to keep the pistons in his knees pounding. The others were nowhere in sight, so Dick slammed the door shut on the cold, reaching hands.

The door latched, but he wasn't sure it was locked.

Dick said, "Look alive, you dildos, or we won't be for much longer."

Johnson got up first and scattered boxes off one of the metal shelves. The cardboard busted, and video cassette tapes clattered across the floor. Despite the thunder of dead hands pounding the door next to his ear, Dick shook his head, wondering why anyone still stored tapes.

Willy took a little longer to rouse from the floor, but he helped Johnson ram the shelf into place over the door. The zombies outside kicked against it, showing they weren't giving up and the shelf wasn't enough. Johnson tossed a few of the busted boxes back on the shelf for weight. Willy knocked cases loose on the next shelf, revealing DVDs and Blu-Rays.

"Hurry up," Dick growled. His eyes darted into every shadow, feeling sure the open door meant some of those things were already inside with them.

Johnson jammed another box into place at Dick's hip as Willy made the next empty shelf scream across the floor. As tapes dumped out of a split along one cardboard corner, Dick grabbed hold, desperate to keep the load in place. His thumb tilted one of the tapes so that he could read the title: *Granny Panty Pool Party Bang*. The copyright was 1987—remastered 1994. Dick grimaced. He was glad the box cover was missing on this one.

Johnson pulled back long enough to join Willy in sliding the next shelf into place. The three of them pressed hard. Sweat stung Dick's eyes. Willy pulled out to toss piles of DVDs and Blu-Rays back on the shelf. Not knowing what else to do, Dick went elbow deep, shoving the movies against the door to make room for Willy to pack in more. Titles flashed past his face as Dick kept pushing: *Too Big Not To Share Seven, Bi Curious Ass-tronaunt Jam: All the Way to the Moon and*

Back, and Dick swore he saw *Midget Strippers versus Hungzilla: the Adventures of the Butt Warriors*. All those titles seemed kind of clumsy to him. Which titles actually got rejected? he wondered.

The undead gathered at the windows along the other wall. With the dark tinting, Dick thought there was no way they could see in, but he'd quickly discovered that the hungry dead had a way of sniffing out the living. The windows strained and began to crack from the edges toward the center. Most windows in this part of town were impact resistant because of the storms, but Dick had learned the hard way that did not usually mean "zombie proof."

"Hold it," Dick said.

Willy used both hands but looked up with eyes wide. "I can't do it. It's too hard."

"You have to," Dick said as he and Johnson ran for the front of the warehouse. "We have to block these windows. Just hold out. Don't blow it until we're ready."

"Help me unload these," Johnson said as he cast aside a box labeled *Put It in Your Mouth Five: the Uncut Version Now with Extra Footage.*

"No. No," Dick said. "That's no good. We have to brace the windows. Leave the boxes on and help me slide it into place."

Johnson showed his teeth. "It's too much. We won't be able to take it all."

"We have to."

They both started to push. The shelf rocked and threatened to bury them, but then groaned across the floor as they moved, inch by inch, toward the windows. Another box toppled from the top and exploded on the concrete floor between them. Copies of *Bear and Twink Picnic Eight* and *Whips and Chains Make Good Neighbors Three: The Foreclosure* spilled around their feet. Dick kicked the movies aside to keep from slipping and wondered why those two titles were boxed together.

They pressed the shelf against a set of the windows and steadied it to keep it from tilting.

"I'm going to lose it back here," Willy shouted.

"Just hold on. We need to finish up here."

Dick said, "We better go faster. We're getting it from both ends."

They took the next shelf and started sliding it across the floor with the same deafening drag. Dick couldn't hear the zombies or see past the boxes in front of him. His eyes danced over the labels: *Christian Spanking: A Hardcore Guide to Sexy Discipline and Holy Matrimony; Tantric Bike Club: Satisfaction On Wheels – The Long Ride; Screwed By Trump: Republican Circle Jerk.*

Dick's head spun. This warehouse seemed to serve some very specific audiences. As they forced the next shelf over the remaining windows, he dropped to his knees and gasped for breath. He couldn't keep going like this, and those monsters weren't giving up.

Willy screamed, and the door blasted open, folding the nearly empty shelves in half. He tried to crawl away, but the twisted metal fell on his legs and pinned him in place as the naked, leaking bodies crawled over the top of him.

Dick and Johnson ran toward him, knowing they were probably too late. More dead swarmed through the gap in the door and over the top of Willy. Reaching through the shelves, they drove their fingers in and then stretched to use their teeth. They pulled him apart in gooey strings. As fluids spread and splattered the floor, Willy never stopped moaning and screaming.

Both men pulled up short and stared, without a weapon in their hands to fight off the zombies or to end Willy's misery.

The glass behind them shattered, and boxes tumbled

from the shelves as their protection failed. Messy creatures lifted off Willy's body and stalked the remaining two.

They ran back through the warehouse.

"What now?" Johnson shouted over his shoulder.

Dick spun and grabbed the edge of a shelf. He tipped it, dumping boxes into the path of the creatures that pursued them. The front of the horde slipped and fell on *Pizza Delivery Sausage Party: The Box Set* and *All Covered in Your Love: The Collector's Edition.*

The undead flanked them in the aisles on both sides. They ran into the darkness deeper in the back. The outline of an exit sign above the door hung dark and black, since the city power had died and the back-up batteries on the warehouse emergency lights were depleted.

"I don't know what's out there," Johnson sputtered, out of breath.

"We have no choice. Go for it."

They hit the crash bar together at a full run and staggered out into the blistering heat and blazing sunlight. As their vision adjusted, they saw the wandering dead turn their milky eyes to the commotion the two of them created. The dead poured out the back door behind them, all sticky from Willy and ready for more.

Dick and Johnson went for the opening between bodies and tried to keep going, even though they were exhausted. Dick glanced over and saw Johnson had grabbed one of the video cassette tapes. As Johnson shoved it into the back of his waistband, Dick read, *Big Beautiful T Girl Dick-tectives Packing the Heat.*

Dick turned his eyes forward as they ran. He tried not to judge. They had bigger worries at the moment than what Johnson might be into on the side. Even so, it really bothered him to think Johnson still had a VCR.

CURSE OF LIGHT AND SMOKE

He drew the pack upward through the night. The light off the three-quarter moon bristled the fur along his back, making the cold feel more bitter. Snow would fall soon. He could smell it and feel it in his bones, still stiff from the slumber of the day and the aching transformation at dusk. He knew he could think better during the day—slower but more deeply. At night, he could move, but everything was passion, hunger, anger, fear, and every limit of emotion, with none of the softer colors in between.

Some nights, he wished he could remember his name. At times, it almost came to him during the slow days, when thoughts and wisdom flowed like sap. During the night, he remembered nothing except how he felt and the danger of those who hunted them even after all these centuries of cursed existence. He did not remember his name nor his crimes against nature worthy of this curse.

He wished every night that he remembered her name. She ran beside him and drew blood with him—for food and fight—until her lighter fur was splashed with gore, her snout stained, and her teeth bared. He did not feel fear when he saw her like that but only the passion. He remembered loving her in passion—and in the subtle colors in between—before the curse took them both. He would give anything just to remember her name. Maybe it was a blessing to live longer with her through this tortured existence.

Her muscles pumped up the mountain, and her energy spurred him on with the pack following. Snow was coming, and ordinary mortals would cut them down during the day if they stayed in the lowlands into the winter. Even the ones not hunting them for who they were would unwittingly take them for what they thought they were.

Dawn broke quickly on the mountain height. The change came on them all with gut-wrenching suddenness. Some still fell to the ground and curled with it, but he had learned to stretch to have it finished sooner. He always stayed close to her so they might stay rooted together through the slow days.

The fur retreated to raw flesh, which stretched long and slender as bone broke apart within him and then dissolved completely. His flesh bruised with hard, grooved bark, and branches sprouted from his body like deformity and tumors. He became a tree with the rest of his grove and with her firmly rooted next to him.

As thought returned to him deeper and slower, he realized the other trees at this point on the mountain slope were white and speckled black. His grove was darker. If any hiker or trapper wandered by, they would stand out and be quite a curiosity. Nothing to be done about it now. They would need to travel higher the following night before they were far enough. Maybe nowhere was far enough, but they were cursed with fur and bark and not blessed with wings or feathers, so the top of the mountains was the best they could do.

Images of the past slipped through whatever consciousness he had during the days without eyes or brain. Castles. No context, but he remembered their shapes and lines in stone. He felt the weak sunlight feed into his leaves. It was small nourishment—he would be famished when darkness returned fur and hunger to him. Fields of grain. Endless. Extending forever over flowing hills. It was food and it was work. He had been small, and the stalks were higher than his head when he was in them. Fire took them. It took the grain and ... lives. He felt the wind move his top as his trunk held firm. He felt her stiff branches brushing his as they moved together and apart.

Rachel.

He pondered on that word for a long time. His name was nowhere to be found, but her name had finally come to him. He felt as much joy as he could at the grand discovery of her name while scarred from root to twigs in bark.

The day grew dark, and he felt a change. No fur, though. It was slow. Confusing. Eyes and face formed partially on his trunk. The day was dark, and this happened sometimes. He could not speak or move, but he could sense while still having the better mind of his daytime form. He smiled and looked up into the dark daytime sky.

Something was wrong. The black cloud cover moved too swiftly, and it was laced with sparks. It stank of carbon.

He turned his eyes in the slow way he was able. The fire line climbed the mountain in an orange blade of death. His slow senses saw the line jump in time as it moved faster than he could process.

The others were afraid. He could not turn to see them all, but he could feel it off the grove. He slid his eyes around in their wooden sockets and looked into her partially formed features. Rachel was terrified.

He could not save her. He could not protect her. The

full understanding of it drove him insane. He drew back into himself so he would not witness her end. He would not watch it all come apart. Not now. Not for Rachel.

He coughed as the smoky darkness of cursed day gave way to the true darkness of frigid night. He curled against Rachel in the ash on the slope as they shivered together, their fur spiked with cold and fear. The trees around them, both light and dark, were charred black and blistered. The rest of the grove was gone, and now they were a pack of two.

Rachel rose first and moved a few paces away. She looked back at him, not in fear but in determination. They needed to go. They had to find other trees to be between on another part of the mountain, away from the wounds of fire, away from those who still hunted them in night and in light. They were both still alive and still together, as much as they could be under this long curse of light and smoke.

He stood because she stood, and he could run because she ran. Eventually, she would let him know it was time to eat, probably after they were within unburned forest again. A place they would not have to remember the loss.

He felt better running. Running with her. He wished he could tell Rachel her name just so she, too, could hear how beautiful it sounded.

END OF THE SEASON

Jill didn't used to be able to see the front of the Chinese restaurant from her porch, but so much of the town had vanished, and the distances between things were screwed up. A teen without his shirt on sat outside and squeezed packets of orange duck sauce into his mouth. The cardboard box of the complimentary packets sat on the concrete beside him.

Jill couldn't tell if he had broken in or if the hinges on the door had simply erased along with so much other detail about the world. He alternated and tilted his head back to drain a packet of soy sauce into his mouth. How was he downing that stuff without water to drink? The supermarket that used to be next door was gone, except for a few thin lines that marked where the corners and windows used to be. She imagined the bottled water had winked out with it.

Jill heard the radio behind her pulse through dead static like the signal was an undulating wave. She imagined cosmic signals humming off the dead, white emptiness that extended out from her home and into eternity in every direction. It was like a blank page that followed the curve of space and folded back upon itself.

Where the back of the Chinese restaurant used to be,

she could see the severed tops of trees. They had lost their roots and most of their trunks. What remained was dimensionless line drawings and the crosshatch of shading. It wouldn't be long until that forest was completely erased and forgotten. For all she knew, that was the last forest left on the planet. She wished then that she had cut down a few of those trees before they mysteriously erased. Wood would have been useful. Any food that had been in the freezers, if the power had still been on, was lost with the back of the restaurant, so the kid was eating condiment packets.

She wanted to invite him across, but they both knew he would fall into the great white void between them. Their chance to team up had passed. They were on islands across a deadly blank page of the universe.

Jill wondered again what caused it. She had that sinking doubt of her own existence. Was all of her life some story or sketch in the imagination of a higher creature? Was that creature erasing its work to start over with the blank page? Her universe was the mistake, and she was no more alive to her creator than a child's doodles. A few more strokes of cosmic rubber and a sweep of the monster's hand, and she, the Chinese restaurant, and the shirtless boy would be gone. Maybe the universe never really existed at all, and this Great Erasure was how it was always destined to end.

The kid squeezed hot mustard into his mouth, and Jill winced. The edge of the sidewalk lost its color and detail. The kid tried to pull his leg back, but he was too late. His shoe, along with the foot inside, had faded away.

Jill turned away and stepped inside. She couldn't watch it happen again.

She took a deep breath and disassembled the table—every bolt and screw—before putting it back together again. The radio hissed and undulated on the static with its soothing music of the blank page outside. As she tightened the screws, the table became more solid. The floor and wall around it regained some of its color.

Jill moved down the hall and opened the cabinet under her sink. Every bottle was empty. She went to the guestroom and dug through the closet. Elmer's glue, glitter, and sunscreen … It wasn't much, but it would have to do. She poured it all into a bucket and mixed the muck with a craft stick.

She took a small paintbrush and smeared the glittery paste over her walls. The edges defined themselves again, and the floor became less spongy under her feet. She tried to make the coat thin so she could cover as much of the house as possible. She wasn't sure what to do once all of this was gone. This trick couldn't possibly work forever. Her house was the last one left in town—maybe the last one in the whole world. Why had no one else figured out how to hold the lines and fight back against the erasures?

Jill paused at her window. The Chinese restaurant had gone flat and was reduced to mere outline. It seemed farther away again. A flat sketch of a boy on the sidewalk tried to lift its head but failed. Jill blinked on tears.

The radio went silent behind her. Jill felt a wash of cold fear and did not want to turn around. It might have been dead batteries, but the kitchen might be gone too. She was exhausted but feared if she closed her eyes, she might never open them again. Breathing used to be so much easier. It was either a problem with the air or with her lungs. There would be no more new days, just blank sky with no sun to rise or set. Jill felt a pang of hunger but tried not to think about the fact that there was nothing left to eat, even if the kitchen was still there.

She smeared her desperate paste over the thinning

glass of the window. There was nothing left to see outside anyway.

"MAYBE NEXT YEAR"

Sheldon didn't want to watch, but he couldn't seem to look away as the third kid jumped off the tower. It was some sort of cell tower on top of an office building perched on a hill. They had gotten past whatever locked barrier was meant to prevent kids from climbing up there. Then they jumped, one by one, off the high side so they fell all the way down the sheer side of the hill to the parking lot of a pharmacy. There was a grassy stretch before the parking lot, with some ornamentals that Sheldon could see in the shadow of the alley where he stood. The third kid missed those and hit concrete. He saw the impact before the sound carried to Sheldon's ear a split second later. That kid wasn't moving any time soon, nor the bodies on either side of him.

That pharmacy was empty. Sheldon had checked it weeks ago. Every pill and scrap of food was taken. He was chased out and followed for several blocks by kids armed with knives and pipes. For all he knew, it was the same kids jumping off the cell tower now.

The next girl leaned out from the top of the tower just below one of the signal dishes. She waved to the world below, and Sheldon fought the mad urge to wave back. She lifted one leg off the crossbar and kicked her foot into open space a few times like a dance move. The boys hanging on behind her shoved against her back and laughed. She managed to keep her grip, though.

Sheldon took his eyes away and checked the bag on his hip. He knew what was in there, but he could not resist the urge to check again. He counted using the sharp edges of the foil as markers. Seven blister packs of the medication.

That was a miracle find. They had stopped making this stuff, and most other medicines, early in 2017. It was only June, but everything was getting tougher to find already. Even food was more scarce than it had been even a month ago. Sheldon tried not to think what it would be like by the time winter came again. Feeding and treating people had dropped off the radar of society. Civilization couldn't hold out much longer, even if the people could.

He thought about the billionaires running Washington. Sheldon wondered if they still sat in their offices or if they stayed in bunkers full time now. Even they couldn't be blamed for what the world had become, could they?

He rubbed the sharp edges of the blister packs with the pad of his thumb and tried not to think about it, tried not to calculate how soon the meds would be used up. Five weeks. The math came out to five weeks. Maybe a little longer if she alternated between suffering and relief by rationing.

Sheldon shook his head and drew his hand out of the bag again. He gripped the strap over his chest with both hands and stared forward. "I don't know what to do anymore."

The girl finally jumped, and Sheldon couldn't help but watch. She twisted as she fell and flipped over twice. Her limbs whipped around her body like she danced in the air or fought against the wind. Something in her movements — or how she pushed off the tower — sent her out from the parking lot and onto the street beyond. She bounced off the pavement as blood splattered around her, and a truck with a welded grill clobbered her in the air. The truck fishtailed but regained its bearing and roared forward without stopping. She tumbled across the lanes and into the ditch on the other side of the highway. Sheldon swore he heard her laughing.

The next boy stepped out on the edge of the tower and gave a shrill whistle over his fingers.

Sheldon turned away and followed the backs of the buildings deeper into the city. "And we thought 2016 was bad …"

Sheldon heard gunfire as he prepared to cross the street, so he crouched and waited. He shook his head. "Why bother?"

The shots echoed and drew closer. He only saw their legs as they broke into the open a few blocks down. Handguns roared, and the slugs rang off of brick walls and the street. He wasn't sure whether anyone was hit or whether it mattered. A shotgun exploded, ratcheted, and blasted again. Someone fell to the street. Sheldon couldn't see the face of the victim, but if that blast peeled off enough of the skin, they would wake to find themselves as a permanent exposed skull, unable to heal any more than that. The eyes would come back, so they would see and feel all of it. He wasn't sure why that mattered to him, but it still did.

"Where are you idiots even finding bullets to waste?"

Sheldon stood and made the run across the street to the next alley. More shots rang out, but none at him. He hoped the gunfire might keep others hunkered down so he could get home quicker. The bullets wouldn't kill anyone, but fear from earlier times when they used to kill still had an instinctive reaction over some people. There were fates worse than death, Sheldon supposed.

Some people feared pain even more now that death was no longer an option. Others were more like those kids jumping off the tower.

Sheldon slipped through the missing side door of a restaurant he used to like. He stepped over the flipped tables and paused at the shattered front glass. He spotted movement up around the third level of the fire escape, one down from his mother's apartment, and thought it might be another thrill-seeking kid performing fear jumps again.

He recognized Mr. Dalton, a veteran from the Vietnam War, maybe sixty on his way to seventy years old. He lived in the unit below Sheldon's mom, and he hung by his neck over the railing buck naked, facing the street below. Mr. Dalton touched himself with furious energy until he blacked out again and his arms went limp.

Sheldon sighed. The man's head lolled at an angle that made him look quite dead with the rope pinching deep into his throat like that.

"You should be so lucky," Sheldon whispered.

He looked to his right and spotted a message in dry blood on a surviving section of the plaster from the crumbling wall. It read: There's always next year.

Sheldon tried to remember if that had been there before.

He looked both ways and crossed the street. Sheldon jumped to grab and pull down the ladder. He moved up two levels and stopped where Mr. Dalton and his wrinkled butt swayed right at face level. Sheldon felt tempted to untie the man and let him wake up in a heap on the sidewalk below, but he decided it wasn't his business. Mr. Dalton had been a kind and helpful neighbor to Sheldon's mother the previous year.

He climbed to the fourth level and entered through the window. "Mom."

She did not answer, but he could hear her breathing.

He popped one of the pills loose and forced it past her sallow lips. Some of the tepid water spilled down her cheek onto her sheets, but she finally responded with a swallow and opened her eyes. She coughed hard enough to shake her entire frame, but she kept the pill down, and the fit subsided.

Sheldon smiled, but his eyes went to the remaining water bottles on the dresser.

His mother followed his line of sight. Nothing got past her, even like this. "You'll have to go to the river again soon and boil some more on the roof."

Nothing left in the water could kill them, of course, but everything could cause pain, and that was the devil in the details now.

"It'll be fine. I'll take care of it. I found a lot this time. We'll be good for weeks. That will buy us time to find more."

She let out a laugh that rattled in her throat, and she gave a slow blink. "Time, we have. Rest, I need. Real rest."

Sheldon nodded and bowed his head over his lap. "If I could make it all stop for you—really end—I would. You know I would do that for you if I could. I'm sorry you have to live with this."

She touched the top of his head. Her hand shook, and he felt hard knobs of bone against his scalp through the thin flesh of her gnarled fingers. He did not lift his head to look. Her joints must have been fiery pain by that point. It had to rival the pit of pain from the tumors in her gut. He wondered if there was still any blood flowing through her hands or if they just continued to operate beyond all logic and reason like everything else in the world.

Her hand fell away from his head and back down to the bed. She said, "Maybe someday. Maybe."

"Do you really believe that? You think maybe the

curse will lift in 2018?" He raised his head but stared at the wall instead of looking at her.

"If enough people wish for something, it's possible to reshape the world."

Sheldon shook his head and buried his face in his hands with his elbows resting on his knees. He closed his eyes.

The fire escape rattled outside. Mr. Dalton was conscious again, it seemed.

Sheldon said, "If wishing made it so, we'd all be free to die again. Everyone in the world must be wishing for it by this point. If the TV and Internet were still up, I'm sure it would be all anyone would ever talk about. That and being hungry all the time."

"Everyone begged for death to stop last year." Something wet gurgled in the back of her throat with each breath. "Maybe we just need a little more time to really appreciate it before we get that gift back again."

Sheldon kept his eyes closed as her breathing went slow and even again. She was out. A few seconds later, the fire escape went silent as Dalton passed out again.

Sheldon needed to get more water. He needed to find food too. It was easy to forget to eat now that people could survive without it, but he felt it was important to keep up the habit.

He listened to his mother's slow breathing a while longer and wished for it to stop. He prayed for the mercy of silence and peace for her at last. Her breathing continued, though, but still he waited and hoped.

The fire escape rattled again. Gunshots popped off in the distance, and someone shouted loud enough to echo off the buildings a few streets over.

Glass shattered somewhere below, and someone laughed. "Gonna pull that thing off, old man."

Mr. Dalton growled outside. "Leave me alone. Mind your own damn business, you punk."

Sheldon was amazed the guy could still speak with the set-up he had going.

His mother's breathing continued, slow and excruciating.

Sheldon stood. He bent down to kiss her forehead gently so as not to wake her up. Then he gathered the empty bottles from the floor around the bed to take to the river for refill. Sheldon stuffed them into the satchel on his hip and left the medicine on the side table near her head. He wasn't sure she could get them out of the packs herself, so he popped two pills loose and left them where she could reach but maybe not knock them on the floor. Maybe.

"Maybe next year," Sheldon whispered.

He turned away from her and stood by the window, watching Mr. Dalton below. Sheldon decided to wait for the man to pass out again before he climbed down past him.

THE LAST SURGERY OF DOCTOR FROST

He did not think he would wake up again, and he was surprised when he did. He stared up into blue sky, with only the scant wisps of clouds to clue him in that he saw this scene in the real world. Alive. Still.

It could have been a warm day back home. The humidity wasn't high enough for it to be the riverfront in summer. It would still be the main property, with the shutters open and furniture uncovered. The long drive with the brick edging. No more leaves to worry about, but the grass would need cutting whether the family was there or at the river house. He liked the grass cut in rows in both directions. Little Scott called it Alice's checkerboard, like in his Wonderland picture book.

He felt boiling hot, though. He tried to remind himself that this might be a fever. He might be in trouble. Infection.

No.

No.

He shivered. It was cold. Deathly cold. He stared up into clear skies and realized he felt hot because his body temperature dropped. Dropped too much, probably.

He still lived because the cold consumed him as he

bled out.

Jeff Frost lifted his head and stared down into his open belly. He needed a rib separator, and he needed a wider incision. Higher. Probably would do to crack the sternum too.

He reached up with a bloody index finger and checked the oxygen tube in his own nose. His hand felt dead and icy. Jeff stretched to his right and fumbled his way up the canister to the valve. The thing didn't want to turn. His own weakness betrayed him, or the bolt had frozen solid.

"Try. Just try," he said, not for the first time. He pictured his son reaching for a book he wanted on a shelf

His son's name was Scott. Scott was five and had eyes the color of the blue sky above the icy plain where Doctor Frost bled. His mother's eyes. Jeff remembered little Scott's last hug before bed. Jeff left the next morning before dawn while Scott was still sleeping. Carol was as well, so Jeff didn't see their blue eyes again the morning he left.

The grass needed cutting, but he'd have to pay someone for that once he returned.

The hug had been different. It was only by a few seconds, really, but it was longer than normal. Jeff didn't say anything extra after goodnight and a kiss on top of the boy's clean hair. Scott rested his head on his father's chest that extra couple seconds.

He didn't ask where Daddy was going, nor when he would be back. He'd probably ask Mommy a hundred times. He might be asking her now, for all Jeff knew.

It was only a couple of extra seconds. A five-year-old seeking reassurance, maybe? Daddy is real. Daddy is here. Maybe it was a glitch in the boy's internal timer that threw off the routine by a mere couple seconds. A minor operational error. Self-correcting. Maybe nothing more.

Jeff was having trouble tracking mental time at the moment, that was for sure.

"Try."

Still, Jeff had the impression it was something else that went unsaid between them, the impression that the boy was afraid to let go.

He fought it, and the valve twisted finally. The effort constricted his stomach muscles, and he felt his guts shift in the open incision. The raw pain that traveled up his center from his balls to the base of his skull felt like a corkscrew inside him. Everything felt wrong. Both tight and loose at the same time.

The airflow weakened. He'd turned the damn thing the wrong way. Dr. Frost twisted the valve wheel three squeaks the other way before it froze up again. Cold oxygen blasted up into his sinuses, drying them out for a moment. Wide open. He'd run out sooner, but what the hell? He needed the kick to the brain. Feed the cells.

"We're all slowly burning to death in a sea of oxygen."

He needed someone else to perform the damn surgery.

At the very least, he needed two other people to assist. Even that Commie in Antarctica had two scientists assisting before he won the Iron Cross for taking out his own appendix.

The rest of the crew died in the crash, so Frost had to do this alone … and no man could repair his own spleen. No one. Not possible. Packing himself with snow was going to have him dead of hypothermia even if it did buy him time to sew himself up.

His hand shook as he lowered the cauterizer. He tried to steady himself. No luck. He went into the laceration anyway. Frost screamed and convulsed. His cries echoed across the cracked ice sheet, which extended into forever beyond the fuselage and one broken wing jammed into the snow past his boots.

He saw black spots, and his eyes teared up once his hand traveled halfway across the field of surgery. He shook his head to clear the moisture and felt the tears freeze to his cheeks. Light flashed in his vision from the synapses blasting inside his skull caused by the overload of pain. He stared down as he continued to traverse slowly with the tool.

Smoke rose out of his belly. Actual smoke with the steam of what was left of his body heat.

A quick glance into the blue sky. We're all slowly burning to death in a sea of oxygen.

Try.

He had to finish.

Even if he could lock down the spleen, which he doubted, he still had to deal with injuries to his intestines.

Done.

He dropped his head back into the snow to stare up into the sky.

He needed to stay conscious. If nothing else, he had to close himself up. He probably was about to die anyway. Maybe repairing the intestine wouldn't matter, ultimately. Either he'd be rescued or he wouldn't. That's what this really came down to.

They were downed in a remote area, through a storm and off course. Radio and transponder out. He had considered getting a Breitling watch like the aviators and astronauts always wore. It had a mini transponder inside that reached out a few nautical miles over clear view like the ice sheet. Maybe ninety miles even? Probably not all the way to the water, but still.

It felt like an extravagance for as seldom as he flew on missions. He remembered holding one in his hand in that little shop in Boston when they went on the Fourth. It had a twenty-four-hour dial just like the ones the astronauts wore in the sixties.

He had bobbed his hand, deciding whether to buy it, but ultimately set it down. He had been so proud of himself for not spending the money, like it had been a great personal victory. The aviator's watch with the transponder inside stayed in Boston. He saved his money to pay for his yard to be mowed in rows for Alice and the Queen to play checkers.

"Clear fucking skies now, though," he said and watched his breath break apart above his face.

No one was going to find him in time. He felt as dead as the rest of the crew, broken apart like his own breath.

Probably would be found by accident. It would be years later … maybe decades. Climate change would break up the already thinner ice miles east. Cutter ships would muscle through the weakened ice. Someone would spot the bits of wreckage and send a crew. It probably wouldn't even be Americans—they stood decades behind in the "Ice Race." Maybe Canadians. Probably the Chinese or Russians, though, who already had nuclear powered ice breakers. The pictures of emaciated bodies would hit whatever version of the Internet existed a half century in the future. The real puzzle would be why the flight surgeon went crazy and started cutting himself up in the snow. It would make all the listicles of strange and disturbing discoveries.

Maybe he'd get lucky and melting ice would send the whole thing to the bottom of the drink. Entombed forever. Buried by rising temperatures they were sent to map from the sky.

God, he was hot. He wanted to strip off some layers.

How many people ended up naked and dead in the snow from hypothermia? Or while accidentally locked in some meat locker? Mistaking freezing to death for burning. He glanced up at one of the wisps of cloud again.

Jeff growled and forced his head off the snow.

He spread his incision and gritted his teeth, then reached in to try and find the nick he had spotted on the intestine. He pulled at the purple, bumpy rope of bowel and felt it in his ass. His stomach lurched. He'd eaten nothing, but he forced the surge back down.

Blood welled and spilt over the side of his belly to absorb into the snow. It spilled again. Too much. Too dark.

He blinked and sucked in a breath of cold oxygen through his dry nose.

Jeff released the intestine and gingerly examined his spleen. It looked like a swollen berry. The thing would have to come out even if his work held long enough to be rescued. No bleeds, though.

Where was it? Why so dark?

His eyes went wide as he felt over the dark surface. His hand came back soaked.

"My liver. Oh, God, my liver."

Jeff shook his head and prodded the thing to find the bleed. If it was too far back, there was no point. He couldn't hold it up and repair it at the same time. There shouldn't have been any way for a man to operate on his own liver anyway, but here he lay.

Liver damage sort of needed to repair itself sometimes. It just needed to be monitored, or there had to be a transplant of one lobe—or the entire liver if the damage was too extensive. That couldn't be an option here.

He found the bleed and reached for his tools.

"Why am I not dead yet?"

Try. Just try, buddy.

"Liver damage is one of the most common internal abdominal trauma injuries," he said.

He watched his breath.

He should have checked the liver first. If he hadn't been on the fool's errand of trying to repair a spleen—

his own spleen—he might have caught it.

"If I had, I would have given up sooner."

He still could.

Jeff shook his head to clear it, but it didn't work. It just made him feel more dizzy.

How long had he been open out in the snow? How much had he bled out?

He should have had bags and bags of blood to transfuse. And an operating room. And a surgical team that didn't include himself.

He went to work. Simple enough in a patient that was hemodynamically stable. Bleeding all the way out was one way to reach stability, he supposed. Unstable patients with liver bleeds were a risky gamble even for skilled surgeons. Most died of it in the early part of the last century. Numbers had improved slightly since then.

Try.

"I'm doing this for Scott ... for Carol. He'll ask when I'm coming home."

Was that true, though? Maybe Jeff needed to believe it was true to keep going, but did he need to keep going?

The spleen wasn't going to hold even if he repaired the liver in time.

"Shit, this hurts."

He continued to work.

If they found him in time, the spleen would still burst as soon as they put him on the stretcher. He'd bet his left nut on it. On his son's bright blue eyes ...

"Just pack it and close. Wait. Hope for the fucking best."

Maybe just slightly better than the fucking worst would do. Was there something worse than operating on your own insides? Dying? Dying might actually be a relief at this point.

Jeff feared to let go. He continued to suture. The liver

was at such a shit angle. His neck hurt. He needed a chair or even a mound of damn snow to hold him up to see. Like repairing every organ wasn't impossible enough. He needed to crane his neck too? How much could reasonably be asked of a person? How much "trying" was enough? When was the damn trial over?

"I've lost too much blood."

Jeff's hands stopped. He waited a beat. Two. Why? He wanted to see if he had the courage to let go, to quit this insanity. If he stopped, it would be over soon. His body was primed for an exposure death. He barely felt the cold anymore …

His hands returned to work. He thought about the feel of Scott's little head on his chest that final bedtime, the feel of his clean hair under Daddy's lips, that extra couple seconds that probably meant nothing.

Jeff lifted his hands and tool away from the damaged lobe of the liver. He waited. No blood. Had his pressure dropped too far at this point, or had he fixed it?

Jeff's hands cramped and went numb, but he used the back of each wrist to pry his fingers apart and to straighten the joints. The liver rested back in place.

He felt along the ropes of his intestines, causing that terrible feeling in his ass again. His balls tightened against his body, and his left testicle throbbed.

"Quit. This is as good as you can do. Close up and hope for rescue. Come on, asshole."

No one is giving you the Iron Cross, Comrade.

He found the nick and gritted his teeth. To come this far and not finish the job—he just couldn't justify that now.

It would be a hell of a thing to be found in fifty years and have them discover he successfully repaired three of his own organs. Oh, the listicles he would make then.

Surgeons deserving of the Iron Cross …

Done.

Done?

He took a deep breath. The oxygen had stopped. Depleted the tank or frozen over. One or the other.

He clawed the tube away from his nose. His fingers smelled like shit. Caked mucus came away with the nose piece.

His nose ran from his right nostril down into his mouth.

Jeff coughed and then gasped. His guts stung.

"Nurse. Kleenex."

He laughed and then groaned.

Jeff blinked several times, then began to close the incision.

He woke up to see more clouds over the blue. Still daytime? Probably, this far north in the summer. Sure, it was.

"Please, mow the snow into rows for me."

The sun hugged the blue sky a little longer than usual—bad internal clock, afraid to let go.

We're on top of the world. Literally.

"I did it, buddy."

For you.

He lifted his head. The incision was closed. He didn't remember finishing. Had he repaired everything or given up?

Maybe he needed to open back up to be sure.

He stared.

The skin around the incision was raw. Red. Hot. Could be from the cold. Probably infection, snow not as clean as he had hoped.

He needed to get out of the cold.

Everything hurt as he tried to shift.

He couldn't feel his legs, though, and they refused to respond. He could drag himself into the cover of the wreckage at least.

He clawed into the snow beside him but had no

strength in his arms to pull after that. His fingers remained buried in the snow as he went back out of consciousness.

In and out. A few times.

The sky took on a twilight glow with the sun closer toward the horizon, behind the largest part of the plane.

Why did he come out in the snow to operate? The cold slowed things down. Slower bleeding. Slower dying. Was that a good thing? A few seconds longer to die than usual?

"Afraid to let go."

Blue sky. Another long day. Cloudless. Nothing to remind a man that he looked into sky instead of a drowning pool. Burning alive in a cold sea of blue oxygen miles deep. A child's imaginings of a sky.

He forced his elbow to bend and drew his left hand out of the snow. Fingers clawed. Black. The nails folded back away from the necrotic, frostbitten flesh of the gnarled fingers.

He lifted his right hand into view for comparison against the backdrop of impossible blue and cloudless sky.

Lighter. Lines of purple and red. Maybe blood poisoning even. Still stained with blood from his own guts. Almost brown or rust colored now. Grey. Dark grey. Frostbite in both hands for sure.

Probably his feet and up his legs as well. Maybe the whole underside of his body.

He felt clumsily at his jacket pockets. He needed a pencil and a paper. He should have spent his last moments writing to them.

What would he have said, though?

Nothing. No pen. No way to leave a note. He could burn it on himself with the cauterizer. No crazier than what he had already done, really, right?

Could he write something in the snow? What?

Something that would hurt them to hear. Even haunt them maybe. Why do that to them?

Best to slip out quietly in the dark and let them sleep.

"You said goodnight the night before. That's good enough … has to be."

He dug through the tools beside him with his right hand. The satchel bumped the empty oxygen canister and tipped it over in the snow.

He used his dead left hand to drag furrows into the snow. He turned the angle of his wrist perpendicular and clawed another set across the first to create a small checkerboard. Two of his fingernails tore off in the snow on the second pass.

He pulled out the bloody scalpel from his satchel with his right hand and brought it to his forehead. The flesh parted easily. Blood ran down his nose into his mouth and tasted salty. He actually felt stronger for it. Warm inside. Like he had just eaten a heavy meal.

He turned the blade and sliced down to the bone across his forehead, creating a disproportioned cross. Something for a god with short legs and long arms.

"Nurse. Sponge, please … Alice, bring the checkers …"

Jeff took out scissors. Not exactly bone flap cutters but good enough for a quick trepanning. Hell, they even did this sort of thing in the Stone Age. People survived it too. Easier than the liver.

The bone crackled, and his stomach tightened on the spot of blood he had swallowed. His insides burned.

He almost lost his nerve.

"Try. Just try, buddy."

Jeff couldn't see the work, but he felt the skull open as he twisted the grips and folded the bone flaps apart in four compass directions. Easier than twisting the oxygen valve. He had a dizzy, light feeling, like he was floating.

He dropped the scissors in the snow without bothering to look. He could use almost anything at that point, but he went for a powered tool. It whirled, and he lowered it into the opening in the center of his forehead. He went slow. Jeff knew if he missed completely or ricocheted off the edge, he might not have the nerve to try again. Not being able to feel his hands didn't help, of course.

Shutter the house and cover the furniture. We're heading to the river.

He didn't get far. An inch, maybe two.

It sounded like running a blender over cream. His hand fell away, and the tool went silent, wedged in the hole and pointing up from his forehead like a unicorn horn.

Thoughts didn't vanish instantly or completely like he expected. He did not die nearly as fast as he'd hoped either. He did forget all those concerns fairly quickly, though.

His lip twitched twice on the left side. A spasm in the left eye, but that passed as well.

His lips moved, but no sound came on the breath, and his breath did not show as vapor above his mouth this time. "Goodnight, buddy."

No clouds in the sky for a point of reference. Nothing to make it seem real.

As Jeff faded, he held on to the blue that was the same color as Scott's eyes, just like his mother's. He didn't understand the blue anymore, but he never took his eyes off it.

BACK IN

They gathered on the lawn like they had done many nights. Jeffery watched the last rays of sunlight burn in the sky, in every color but blue. He missed the daylight and blue sky in the moment before darkness.

Jeffery rubbed at the gash across his stomach—it always itched at night. He felt hungry.

Cameron brushed the dirt off the front of his shirt from the digging and playing. The other boys whispered as they stared up at the house.

Cameron turned. "Who is taking their turn tonight? How about you, Jeffery?"

The other boys breathed out a cold sigh of relief. The sound made him angry.

"You can always take a turn, Cam," Jeffery offered.

Cameron licked dirt out of his teeth. "I went last night, and I brought out the ring, remember?"

Cameron held out his hand, looked around the ground.

"Damn. I dropped it again."

Jeffery shook his head. "I don't think that was last night. No one went last night."

"Who cares?" Cameron yelled. "I went since last time you went."

Jeffery waved his hands at the other boys. "Some of them have never gone back in."

He saw their shoulders tighten. It made him smile. Some of the younger boys covered their faces and started to cry. Jeffery felt angry, but at himself. He saw the scars and cuts through their torn clothes. Some of them were missing fingers. One boy only had a hole where his nose should have been. Jeffery could hear it whistle when he breathed. Even that boy had gone back in since last time Jeffery took the challenge.

"Fine," Jeffery said. "I'll go. What do we want this time? His watch? His glasses?"

"I got his ring," Cameron said. "This time, I challenge you to take something that sparkles when he smiles … unless you're scared."

The other boys let out a long *ohh* sound. Some of the younger boys backed away from the crooked porch.

Jeffery spit in the grass. "I'm not scared."

He pushed past Cameron and walked up the slanted front steps.

Cameron called after him. "Remember to smile. He likes when you smile."

"Shut up," Jeffery said as he pushed through and found himself on the other side of the closed door.

The house instantly smelled like beef and soup, which filled Jeffery with memory and fear. He felt the need to pee even though he had not drunk anything all day. The boards creaked under his feet. He heard something move in the living room. Jeffery took two deep breaths and walked past the door to the basement without looking.

Jeffery had not known Cameron before the murders started. Cameron went in before him. The butcher had snatched Jeffery right out of his own backyard the last afternoon he saw blue sky. Jeffery had stared at the back of his house as the man who smelled like beef clapped his hand over Jeffery's mouth and nose, hauling Jeffery over the fence. He had seen his mother's shape move past the window as the house disappeared behind the trees. She had not seen Jeffery. He was sure. She would have come out screaming, and Jeffery had not heard any screaming until he was on the chain in the basement. The chain had been sticky with other boys' blood. It might have been Cameron's. Jeffery stayed alive in the dark for a long time. Thinking about what the butcher had done to him in the dark before he started cutting made Jeffery feel sick in his gashed open stomach.

"I know you are there," the man yelled from the living room.

Jeffery shook, but he kept walking over the creaking boards.

He looked around the tables, boxes, stacks of newspapers, and spotted what he was looking to find. Jeffery concentrated as he wrapped his small hand around the shiny silver handle. It would not lift for him. He took two deep breaths and tried again. The mirror lifted out of the box. Jeffery looked in it and smiled, but he could not see his face.

Each time the butcher had done a bad thing before and during the cutting, he had told Jeffery to smile. Jeffery's house was not far away from the basement, but he never saw it or his mother again. The butcher buried him in the yard next to Cameron.

Jeffery walked into the living room and saw the man sitting in the chair, wrapped in the blanket. The butcher was older and weaker.

The man looked around without seeing Jeffery and said, "I feel your cold. Stay away. Stay away!"

Jeffery walked through the couch, dangling the mirror behind it so the butcher would not see it.

The man covered his eyes and cried like one of the little boys. One of his ring fingers was a stump.

"I haven't cut in years. I'm sorry. Just kill me or leave me alone."

Jeffery lifted the mirror over his head. "Smile."

The man looked up like he had heard. He screamed instead. Jeffery saw the gold tooth, and it filled his empty stomach with terror. He smashed the edge of the mirror into the side of the old man's jaw until he slumped over.

Jeffery dropped the mirror and picked up the tooth from the spew of blood. He ran back through the house as the man gagged and cried in his chair. Jeffery pushed the tooth under the bottom of the door and ran through.

He held it up in the air, and the boys cheered. Even Cameron. Each one wanted to hold it. Even the little boys. They laughed as they walked to the backyard, then burrowed back into the dirt in each of their spots before morning. As dirt filled Jeffery's ears, he heard the younger boys saying they wanted to try next.

Jeffery felt his stomach fill with earth, relieving his itching and hunger. He clutched the gold tooth and smiled.

DADDY ELVIS AND THE LAST JOB

Miami, Florida, and Conway, South Carolina, might as well have been on two different planets in 1974. There was no respectable path between the two, so even though he swore he never would, Son Elvis packed up after his last show the Tuesday he got the telegram that his father had died, and he hitchhiked north to Atlanta, then due east toward the ocean.

Son performed under wigs, makeup, and the name Sunny E. He wore a ball cap as he hitchhiked through Georgia into South Carolina.

The last guy to pick him up on Highway Twenty was a man who called himself Earnest. They had driven through four exchanges and were headed up a two lane between cornfields.

"You can let me out wherever," Son said. "I don't want to put you out."

"No trouble," Earnest said.

Son shook his head under the ball cap. He expected the old guy was gathering up the courage to murder Son or ask him for a BJ. Son was giving a mental coin flip as to which outcome was more likely. They were close to Conway, so maybe it could be a double funeral. It was Thursday, so he'd arrive just in time for the funeral on Friday. Also, it wouldn't be the first time Son had blown a stranger in a car, but his dad had just died, so he wasn't in the mood for giving BJs or being murdered.

The guy could have been going on to Myrtle Beach, just one town over, so Conway could actually be on his way.

Son asked, "Are you going to the beach?"

"No," Earnest said.

Son sighed. He was going to get murdered just a few miles shy of the hometown he swore he'd never go back to.

"Who's your daddy?" Earnest asked.

For a moment, Son thought this might be a pick-up line, then he got nervous that the man had some kind of hoodoo psychic power. Son remembered he had mentioned the funeral back when he got picked up on Highway Twenty half a state ago.

"Oh, ugh, Frank Elvis," Son said. "He owned Pulp Westerns out on Five Oh One, a country western bar in Conway. He and my mother own it. *Owned* it. And my ex-wife. And my two brothers' ex-wives too, I guess."

"That's a strange partnership," Earnest said.

"Divorces were ugly, and we lost our shares in it," Son said. "My wife got my part first, and then my brothers' wives got the idea from her in their divorces."

"You got divorced first?" Earnest said.

"Yes," Son said. "I'm the oldest. I have to set the example."

"Three brothers, three divorces."

"Like a musical," Son said.

"What caused such a thing?"

Son said, "Irreconcilable differences. We all discovered one by one that we liked different things. Well, I suppose, actually, all six of us liked the same thing, but that didn't really work so well for a marriage situation, as it were."

Earnest glanced over at Son but didn't ask anything else. They pulled into Conway, over the river and up the hill toward Lake Kingston Methodist.

"I'm stopping here at the church," Earnest said. "I can take you over to the bar or drop you off at your mother's house."

"Why are you stopping at the church, Earnest?"

"I'm retired clergy and knew your daddy back when you were still toddling, before your two divorced brothers were born. Your father had in his papers for me to preside his funeral. I think he expected to die younger from getting shot—and probably meant to switch my name out but never got around to it—so your mother tracked me down, and I put in my good speech-making teeth."

By the time the retired pastor finished talking, he had pulled into a space in front of the church.

Son asked, "How did you recognize me on the road?"

"I didn't, but by the time I figured it out, it was too awkward to say anything, so I just finished out the trip. Pulp Westerns then?"

So, it was going to be a BJ, Son thought.

"No, I'll walk," Son said.

They both got out of the car.

"See you at the service tomorrow," Earnest said.

Son backed away a few steps before turning and walking down the hill through the same trees, houses, and businesses that had always been there. The town had not had enough self-respect to change at all.

As he reached highway 501, with tourists creeping across the bridge toward the beach, Son eyed the side of Pulp Westerns just a few feet away. He steeled himself and rounded the building in the empty parking lot to face the closed sign in the window. After a few breaths, he pulled open the exit door and stepped into the darkness.

Three parts of the room moved: his mother spread receipts on the counter and slashed at them with a pen; three women lounged behind the bar folding paper napkins; his two younger brothers slouched over beers at the table in front of him. Something wasn't right about the room, something beyond Son being back in it. He cut his eyes over to the stage and saw the house instruments were replaced by a podium, a blown-up poster of Frank Elvis's face three times life size, and a coffin sized platform.

"You're bringing him into the bar? You serve food here," Son said.

"I'm doing math," his mother said. "Welcome back and shut the hell up a minute."

Son's ex, between the other two Elvis wives, said, "You want a beer?"

"You have anything imported?"

His former wife just stared at him with the same distant stare she had given him the last few years they were together. It chilled his blood like old times. She was never unkind, even when he had confessed his unfaithfulness and then confessed it was with her best friend's husband. He had left town, and she had stayed with his family running the bar.

"Whatever you have cold is fine. Just not the family brew, please. I don't need the squirts before the funeral."

His mother said, "Watch your trap, boy."

Son sat down at the table with his brothers. Long sat to his left, and his younger brother, Stitch, slumped over his empty bottle to Son's right.

"Stitch just lost his boyfriend before coming down from Chicago," Long said.

"The hell does he need to know that for?" Stitch asked.

"Lost?" Son asked.

"Left, not dead," Stitch said.

Long said, "I thought Son should know why you're so sad."

"I would have thought it was because of Dad," Son said.

"That would have made sense," Long said. "He did break up, though."

"Are you dating anyone?" Son asked.

"I live in Conway still," Long Elvis said. "Not many options, gay or straight."

Son's ex set an open Pulp Western Brew on the table and walked away without comment. Son sighed and slid the open bottle over to Stitch, who took it up without a look.

Mother Elvis swept the receipts into the drawer and walked over to the table with the boys. "Is he in?"

"I hadn't asked yet," Long said. "I wasn't sure he was even coming until he walked in."

"Am I in for what?" Son asked.

His mother said, "We need to be making plans. The chitchat can wait."

"In for what?" Son said.

"He just got here, Mom. We need to work up to it."

Stitch said, "They want us to pick up the last haul from Dad's job before he wrecked."

Son looked back and forth between his mother and Stitch Elvis. "I thought Dad died of a heart attack."

"You can't say he was running from the cops and crashed into a school bus in a telegram," his mother said.

"Why not? You think the FBI is checking my telegrams? Just tell me it was a wreck."

"He had the heart attack a few hours later," Long said.

"What job? Was the money in the car with him?" Son asked.

"You know Dad's rule," Stitch said.

"Yeah—Rule Five: Keep the money hidden and keep it moving. He could have been moving it."

"He wasn't," their mother said.

Long's ex set an imported beer in front of Mother Elvis and hit Long on the back of the head as she retreated.

"It's in the basement of the Freaky Deaky," Long said.

Son said, "What's that now?"

"Freaky Deaky is in the old Rivioli Theater. It's a nostalgia club with a Fifties theme," their mother said.

"And there is a haul in the basement Dad died running from the cops for?" Son asked.

"Tell him the rest of it," Stitch said.

"What's the rest of it?"

Long said, "Stickley owns the Freaky Deaky."

Son stared at the table for a few beats.

"I'm staying for the funeral, and then I'm headed back to Miami," Son said.

"We need this take, or we lose the bar and my house," their mother said.

Son said, "Maybe you and our ex-wives will need to move on to something more legitimate."

"Like singing drag in Miami?" his mom asked.

"Yes, something legal like that."

Long said, "Just do this for Mom, Son. Do it for Dad. Do it for leaving me here to carry him through the jobs alone."

"Save the guilt trips. I already have an ex-wife."

A bottle cap bounced off the back of Son's chair from the direction of the bar, but he ignored it.

"That's fine. Did all of your father's Western Union payments make it while you were setting up in Miami? That illegitimate money spend okay among your Cuban boyfriends?"

Son said, "Stitch, are you going to fall back into this dirty money nonsense from when we were kids and had no choice?"

Stitch said, "Yeah, I'm not exactly all legitimate up in Chicago either, Son … and all my Western Union payments showed, so I've already agreed to it."

"I know all the details," Long said. "It's in and out."

"Stickley isn't going to be an easy 'in and out' unless he has us bent over a table," Son said. "What happened to Rule Four: Pick targets based on what's easy for you and tough for them?"

"It was an easy target," his mom said. "He just died before completing the last move, so the haul still sits in the Freaky Deaky basement."

"Does Stickley know it's there?" Son asked.

They didn't answer, and Son stood up. He walked halfway to the door before his mother spoke up.

"Where are you going, Son?"

"I'm going to find somewhere to get a drink."

"We own a bar," Long said.

Long's ex said, "We own the bar; you just drink here."

"I'm going to go somewhere that everyone's not trying to kill me."

His mother said, "Be here early tomorrow morning. We'll need help getting your Daddy from the cooler to the stage."

Son turned around at the door. "He's already here? In the drink cooler? Don't answer that."

Son shut the door—with his family, living and dead, inside—and watched the closed sign swing on its hook.

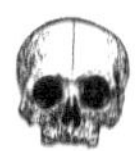

Son stepped out on the porch of Pulp Westerns with music still blaring at his back from inside. The closed sign had been replaced by one that announced "Private Party." Son wasn't sure what was private about it, as he couldn't think of anyone from town who wasn't inside drinking under Frank Elvis's picture, except maybe retired pastor Earnest, who hadn't actually showed for the funeral.

The door opened, hitting Son on the elbow and letting out Long and more music.

"You okay?" Long Elvis asked.

Son pulled the misfit cowboy hat from his head and threw it down on the bench.

"Where's Stitch?"

"He already went to wait for us at the train station," Long said.

"Why are we still here then?"

"I wanted to be sure you had time to grieve," Long said.

Son pulled the hat off his brother's head and threw it down next to the other.

"Dressing up like cowboys for Dad's wake is the gayest thing I've ever done, Long, and I sing drag for a living. Let's go."

Long looked back at the bench with the two hats as they walked away.

"That hat's actually mine. It's expensive."

"Just leave it," Son said. "Dad's rule number three."

"Dress plain," Long said. "What's plainer than a cowboy hat?"

"Everything," Son said. "No cowboy hat. Let's go before I change my mind."

At the small platform for the train station, Stitch handed his brothers a ticket each. They were marked: The Historic Black Swag. No one checked the tickets as they boarded and sat down in a near-empty car behind the engine. The walls and seats were coated with black coal dust from the engine's smoke stack. As the train started rumbling across the marshes, the smoke choked into the car. The other passengers retreated to different cars out of the path of the soot, leaving the three brothers alone.

"Good. Does everyone understand the plan?" Long asked.

"I understand the steps," Son said. "The plan escapes me."

"Is that fancy Miami talk for you do understand or you don't understand?" Long said.

"Why was Dad mixed up with Stickley on a job anyway? Rule number seven was to keep company better than yourself."

Stitch sniffed at the black smoke starting to cake inside his nostrils.

Long said, "Dad was going downhill this last year. By this final job, everybody was better company than him. The bar, the house—everything was at risk if we didn't score big."

"Well, he's dead," Son said.

"I guess we got a chance to make the last bit right now," Long said.

"Dad said you follow the seven rules or you end up dead," Son said. "We should be taking the hint and walking away."

Long said, "This job was the walk away. This was it. If we don't finish it, it will have been for nothing."

"They were all for nothing," Son said. "Every crook says every job is the last job until the funeral. We'll probably end up the same way."

"Sometimes you just have to take one for family, right, Son?" Long said.

Son didn't answer one way or the other, and they rode in silence until they were shaking coal dust out of their clothes, stepping off the Black Swag in Myrtle Beach. They kept to side streets a couple blocks up from the Ocean Front Road. A few homeless guys sat stewing in their sweat and didn't even bother asking the brothers for handouts.

The Freaky Deaky stood a story taller than the buildings around it. Posters for a Shag dance contest hung in the glass cases, and music leaked out of the cracks.

Long glanced at Stitch and Son. Son waited for him to say something to them about the big plan, but he turned away and pushed inside the foyer without a word.

Stitch folded his arms and stood on the sidewalk facing out to the street.

"This is a stupid plan," Son said. "Like following the old man into death kind of stupid. I could come up with a better plan than this, if I was high and drunk."

"I am drunk, and nothing comes to mind," Stitch said. "You seem to remember Dad's rules for responsible thievery well enough. What about six?"

"Don't brag?" Son said.

Stitch said, "No, it's never brag. Never brag, Son. You had all night, the whole train ride, and just now to hatch a master plan, and you didn't. So, never brag. Just go do your part, and let's be on the next train out."

Son turned and walked up the grassy gap between the theater and the hurricane fencing of the abandoned lot next door.

"Not doing this is the better plan."

If Stitch heard, he didn't say anything in response, just stood watch out on the sidewalk as suspicious looking as could be.

Son stopped at the particle board paneling of a storm door that failed to fit its frame. He pulled his tools from his pocket and rolled the plastic pouch open on the ground. He pulled two different sized picks from their slots and then eyed the padlock. As he lifted it up to reach the keyhole on the bottom, he bumped the face of the board with his elbow, and the door swung open on its rusty hinges all by itself. Son looked down at the lock in his fist, which was bound over the metal loop, but the door latch had not been closed first, so the door hung open to the dark stairs leading down into the theater's basement.

Son cursed, gathered up his tools, and walked down into the darkness below the building. The music and dance steps pounded from the floor above. Son flipped on his flashlight, which was as long as his forearm, and scanned through the piles of clutter from the history of the theater.

He spotted two canvas army bags with F. ELVIS stenciled in black on the olive green sides.

"Too easy," Son said.

He knelt down and pulled at the drawstring that closed the top of one of the bags. The cold double bore of a long gun pressed against the back of his head, and he stopped.

"Son Elvis, sorry to hear about your father. I couldn't make the funeral because I had to guard the basement from thieves."

Son lifted his hands as he remained kneeling over the bags with the thundering Shag dancing going on overhead.

"You should lock the door then," Son said.

"People break it, and then we have to put up cheap particle board until the new door can come in from the upcountry. It's better just to run the bums out after they walk in."

"I'll just be running then," Son said.

At least one of the hammers clicked back. Yes, it was definitely a shotgun—not sawed off. Son could feel the nice smooth bore.

"No," the traditional shotgun man said, "we are done getting harassed by Elvis and his queer sons. We cut loose Daddy, and now all his gilded offspring came galloping home just like we expected. At least there won't be any grandchildren, right?"

Son turned around and looked up along the barrel at Ryan Stickley. He had red hair and a pot belly but not the Viking beard of his burly father, who Long was supposed to be distracting upstairs.

"Are you going to shoot me in the basement all over the money?"

Ryan looked between the bag and Son.

"You're lucky I didn't shoot off your face when you surprised me turning around like that, but I guess you are used to that kind of thing, being gay and all."

"Fuck you, Ryan. My dad worked his ass off making your dad rich."

Ryan snorted and pulled back the second hammer on the shotgun.

"Your daddy hasn't earned in years and cost more than brought. Then he comes crawling back, all crazy from booze and begging for work. He screwed up every job he tried," Ryan said. "He probably would have died on his own eventually anyway."

"What did you say?"

"Don't even worry about it. We're going to wait on my daddy's men to bring Long down, and then we'll be most of the way done with the Elvises. Is Stitch outside or waiting at the train?"

"You go to hell, Ryan," Son said.

"You're losing your manners, just like Daddy Elvis did. Rule number one, Son—be polite. Say 'please' and 'thank you.' Now shut your gay mouth until the whole party gets here, or I'll scatter your teeth down your throat. I guess that would serve you just fine with what you do with your mouth, right?"

"I haven't forgotten rule two," Son said. "Back up threats."

Ryan looked toward the stairs. Son took the flashlight

off the floor and swung up as he jumped up from the concrete. The metal tube cracked underneath Ryan Stickley's chin as Son's shoulder lifted the shotgun barrel toward the ceiling. Ryan groaned and coughed, spewing the end of his tongue and a string of blood out into the air. As Ryan staggered, Son brought his fist back down on the Stickley boy's skull, breaking the flashlight open, sending blood and batteries falling toward the floor.

Both barrels fired off through the ceiling and the dance floor above. The dancers screamed and ran while Ryan fell to his back on the concrete.

Son snatched up the duffle bags and ran up the stairs to the alley. As he smashed through the particle board, tearing it off its hinges, the sun dazzled his eyes for a moment.

"Stitch?"

With the bags bouncing heavy off his sides, he ran along the fence toward the street. Stitch stepped out into the mouth of the alley.

"Did you hear a blast?"

Son was out of breath as he reached his brother on the street. Dancers from the contest ran from the doors, out through the street, past the homeless men. Long ran out and grabbed the bags away from Son. He bled down his left sleeve from a cut on his shoulder.

"Let's go. Stickley knew we were coming."

"Yes, I got that," Son said. "Let's find somewhere to hide this and then go. I just bloodied Ryan down the basement."

"Are you cut?" Stitch said, "Who got shot?"

"No one."

"Two dancers," Long said. "We have to get this back home."

"Stickley's going to come for us," Stitch said. "Let's hide it and then hide ourselves. That's the smart move.

Keep money hidden and keep it moving."

Long walked past them up the sidewalk with the scattering crowd.

"We'll get you boys home in time to catch a ride back out of town. Don't worry."

Stitch and Son looked at each other and followed their brother—and the duffle bags—back to the Black Swag. They loaded onto the empty car behind the engine.

"We should find another way back," Son said.

Long set the bags on one of the benches and looked out through the windows.

"You want to walk back home through the swamps?"

"I don't want to wait around here to get caught," Son said.

"Son, Long, we have company," Stitch said.

Both brothers scanned through the windows before they spotted their mother looking through the doorway that led to the engine. The door swung inward, and their mother stumbled forward a few steps before dropping to her knees. The boys took a couple of steps but stopped as Reverend Earnest walked up behind her with a pistol aimed at the back of her head.

"Who the hell are you?" Long said.

Son was about to answer before his mother spoke.

She said, "My cousin Ernie."

"I thought you were the preacher," Son said.

Mother Elvis laughed, and Earnest swatted her on the back of the head with the gun. Long balled his fists and took another step, but Earnest rested the gun back on Mother Elvis's head.

He said, "Get punchy, boy, and its first her, then you. Toss those bags over here, or I start shooting."

"Are you cut?" she said.

Long stared at Earnest without answering.

"I guess when I didn't see you at the funeral, I should have known better."

"Toss the bags," Earnest said.

"Don't shoot in here," Long said. "You'll blow us all up."

Long stepped back and opened one of the sacks. He pulled out a twelve- inch rod wrapped in wrinkled, purple paper.

"What the hell is that supposed to be?" Son asked.

"I don't care what it is," Earnest said. "Give me the money."

"There is no money," Long said. "This was the haul. It's like dynamite, only several times more powerful. The job was to steal this from the logging company and use it to blow open the vaults of all the banks in town before going on the run."

Long opened the bag further and revealed it was full of the purple sticks.

"Are you kidding me?" Son said. "Ryan fired off a shotgun in that basement. We could have blown a hole into Hell."

"What does the B&C company need with that?" Stitch asked.

"Clearing rubble and leveling land," Long said. "They are going to clear the marshes and sell it for real estate. Stickley wanted to sell the explosives to underground anarchists. Dad wanted to do one last job before starting over with new identities. That was the plan. Mom thinks Stickley cut Dad's brakes."

"Lots of people wanted him dead," Earnest said.

"That's why he stopped working with you," she said.

"Watch it, woman."

"You didn't think to share those details before dragging me into this?" Son said.

"Go back to Miami then, Super Star," Long said.

"We should have brought guns," Stitch said.

"Not with explosives around," Long said.

"If you're concerned about our safety, tell us there are

explosives in the bags," Son said.

"Stop fighting," Mother Elvis said.

Earnest raised the gun and pointed it at Long.

"Listen to your mother, boys. Shut up so I can think."

Long held up his hands and waved the purple stick in one fist.

"Don't shoot. You'll blow us all up."

"We'll do the banks together then," Earnest said. "I'll keep her safe. You'll bring the money. Then we split it up and go our separate ways."

"I'm out," Son said.

"He's got Mom," Long said.

"It's too late to be out, Son," Earnest said. "You took the ride, and now you're here. Time to pay the fare one way or the other."

A gunshot sounded, and glass shattered on both sides of the train car. Long and Stitch dropped to the floor. Earnest pushed Mother Elvis down on her face. Three more shots tore through the sides of the train car, sending wood, glass, and foam from inside the seats into the air.

"Stop shooting," Long said.

Earnest dropped to his knees and turned toward the open door leading to the engine.

"Get us out of here, Buck."

A voice said, "This ain't a car. We can't just speed away. Who's shooting?"

"We're being robbed," Earnest said. "Get us gone or we're going to end up dead."

Son still stood in the middle of the car and looked out the broken windows. A bald man with a thick red beard stood out on the other side of the street beyond the train platform with a half dozen other armed men. Daddy Stickley had several guns strapped over his shoulders and aiming skyward. The men fired more shots into the train car. Son felt a couple whiz past him, with bits of shrapnel from the car splintering into his skin. Long called up from the floor.

"Stop," Long said, "we have the purple in here."

"He knows."

Son jumped over his mother and slammed into Earnest's back, knocking him on his face. The pistol went off, and the round rang off the iron of the engine ahead. Son heard shouts over Stickley's men still firing into the second car.

Earnest said, "Get off me, fairy."

Son drove his fist into the back of the man's head and neck, just behind the jaw, in the bad nerve spot his daddy had taught him about when he was younger. Earnest raised the gun up and fired blindly through the roof. Son twisted the pistol out of the man's grasp and slammed it butt-first into the back of the reverend cousin's head three times.

"Thank you," Son said. "Long, get off your damn face and get Momma off the other side of the train."

"They're coming on board," Long said. "Just stay down."

Son rose up and fired two shots through a window frame holding shards of broken glass. One of the men crumpled to the sidewalk. The others scattered for cover, but Stickley didn't budge. He dropped a long gun to the ground by his feet and pulled another one off his back. Stickley fired through the walls along the car in a systematic way without aiming right at Son.

"He's not coming onboard," Son said. "He's trying to hit the stuff. Long, get Mom off the train. Stitch, take the bags out before they get hit. That's a man that backs up threats."

Stitch crawled forward, hissing as his hands came down on the broken glass on the floor of the train. Long got up and ran past his brother, grabbing up the bags himself and heading toward the engine. Stitch looked up at Son.

"Get Momma."

Stitch changed course and pulled their mother up to her knees. She held her belly where a patch of blood stained her dress.

"She's been hit," Stitch said.

"Get her off the train!"

As Long ran, Stickley spotted him and turned his aim back toward the front of the car. He and his men fired shot after shot into the car. Son fired two more shots out at Stickley but missed. Earnest reached up from the floor and grabbed Long's ankle, spilling him onto his face. The bags opened, and the purple sticks rolled out into the debris along the floor. One stick rolled out the open door and came to rest on the connection between the engine and the train.

Stickley smiled through his beard and raised the gun up to his eye to take aim.

"Oh, hell," Son said.

He ran between the seats and leaned out the window to aim back at Stickley. Son pulled the trigger several times, but the gun clicked empty. He looked to his right and saw that his mother and brother had not reached the door yet; he looked to his left and saw Long looking back up at Son, crying.

Son reached down and grabbed up one of the purple sticks. He drew his hand back to throw it out the window at Stickley.

Stickley fired.

The first explosion broke the train and the track. The engine lifted off the rails and rolled to the side. Flame filled the second car and blasted through the doors into the third and fourth cars. The next explosions came one after the other within three seconds and left a crater in the spot where the train station used to be.

Stickley underestimated the power of the last haul,

and a burning wheel from the train car tore through his substantial belly, leaving him on his back looking up at the sky. As he stared at white clouds through black smoke for a few more seconds of consciousness, he heard at least one of his men crying and sirens approaching from the distance.

Stickley thought that at the very least he was rid of the Elvis boys. He tried to smile but didn't live long enough to do that.

THE NIGHT OF THE MULLETED VAMPIRE KILLING BRAT PACKERS

Cammie shoved her brother through a doorway too small for him and the body he carried over his shoulder. Greg struck his head on the top of the doorframe on the way through and lost his balance with his sister still pushing against his back. As he spilled across the concrete floor in the dark, Buddy's body rolled off Greg's shoulder and struck the back of his skull against the leg of the sausage packing machine before bouncing on the floor.

Greg cursed at Cammie, but the word died in the noise of her slamming the door to the backroom of the plant. She turned the locks that had little hope of keeping the spikey-haired vampires out if they spotted the trio.

Greg groaned as he felt for a pulse on Buddy's neck. "I need light."

Cammie snorted. "Eat my shorts, Gregory. We're not shining a spotlight for those bleached-blond bloodsuckers to find us. They've bitten the whole town, and we're the last ones left."

Greg turned and faced his younger sister in the dark. He knew the packing plant like the back of his hand from filling brat sausages day after day. Probably could run the machines in the dark, but he had never been in the building at night with his best friend possibly dying. He wasn't sure what to do even if he had light.

"I can't see, Cammie. I think Buddy is dying."

"Is he bitten?"

"No, he's not bit! Now shut up and help me. I think he hit his head."

Cammie stood on her toes to look out the bottom edge of the barred windows. "Are you sure? They were all over us. If he's bit, we have to deal with it."

"He's not bit."

"He wouldn't want to become like one of those things out there, with their mullets and their savage lack of morality in a town that does not follow up well on missing children reports."

"I'm not killing my best friend, Cammie. I'm not."

Cammie turned. With her back to the wall below the window, she tilted her head and stared at the scarred wood of the door.

"Greg, he made me swear not to let him become one of those monsters with their shirts off playing saxophone for no reason."

Greg looked up at his sister in the dark. "When did he say this? We've been running all night."

"While you were downstairs making stakes out of chair legs, we did it upstairs. I gave him one of my diamond earrings, and we talked afterward."

Greg covered his face. "You mean did it like *it* it? Oh, gross, Cammie. Is that what that weird, swelling music was that had no lyrics?"

She shrugged. "We didn't want you to hear us—he was supposed to be standing guard—and I like that music."

"Yeah, the vampires caught the house on fire and we had to run, Cammie. Remember? Okay, let's kill him just to be safe."

"Wow, Gregory," she grabbed his shoulder, "is this because you think he's a vampire or because he scored with your sister?"

"Get your hands off me, Cammie. I know you haven't washed them."

She let go of her brother's shoulder.

He reached down and felt Buddy's earlobe. Greg found the earring and tore it loose.

Buddy sat bolt upright and gasped for air. Greg staggered backward, and Cammie jumped in Buddy's lap, kissing his neck.

Greg turned his back. "Are you going to do him again, Cammie? You want me to turn on a few machines for some cover noise?"

Buddy pushed Cammie away and crawled under the machine behind him. "I have to go back."

Greg spun back around, looking for Buddy. "Where did he go? What are you talking about? My house is burned down. You know that."

Buddy pulled out his pocketknife and sawed at the cord to the industrial packer. "I have to go back. I didn't find the answer, but I think I can with just a little more time."

Cammie knelt and looked at Buddy's back under the table. "Back where, Buddy? What do you mean?"

The blade sliced through the insulation and copper, sending sparks off the end of the knife. Buddy hissed.

Greg pushed the machine, creating a loud screech as he revealed Buddy squatting by the broken piece of cord still in the outlet.

Greg narrowed his eyes. "How did you cut through an industrial wire with a pocket knife?"

Cammie looked up at her brother. "We're being chased by vampires with mullets, and this is the part you can't believe?"

"It's a thick wire filled with metal fibers," Greg said. "It's just unlikely a pocket knife would do it, is all I'm saying."

Buddy separated the bundles of copper with his fingers, cutting himself with the sharp ends. "I'll need you to try to bring me back if this is going to work."

Greg opened his mouth to speak, but he froze as Buddy touched his tongue to the wires still connected to the outlet. Power laced up through Buddy's body, arcing out in uneven light. Greg would swear he saw Buddy's skeleton for a split second.

Buddy toppled back into Cammie's arms with tendrils of smoke rising out of his mouth. Cammie screamed.

Greg pulled Buddy away from Cammie by one of his arms and laid Buddy out on the concrete, then began compressions on his friend's chest.

Cammie covered her eyes. "Why did he do it?"

Greg pointed. "You get to blow in his mouth. I don't know where that's been."

The door splintered behind them, sending shards of wood across the concrete. Cammie screamed as Greg turned to look. Through the two breaks in the door, he saw glowing red eyes and acid washed jeans with a pink bandana wrapped around the knee.

Greg breathed. "Kip."

Black claws tore away the openings in the wood as Greg pulled Buddy's body back onto his shoulder.

"Come on, Cammie. We have to get out of here."

Buddy jolted awake on the thin carpet with his back to the plaster wall. He still did not know where he was, but more students had filled the desks of the lecture hall since last time he appeared there.

He had no way of knowing how much time had passed.

Buddy staggered to his feet and walked up behind the same girl he had spied on last time. He heard his breathing echo like the sound of being trapped inside a tin can.

She still had her computer opened. The device was impossibly thin, like a notebook with moving pictures. She was connected in with wires and tiny plugs attached to both of her ears.

Buddy whispered in a sharp echo, "This must be the future."

She turned and looked at him. The girl screamed, stumbling away, pulling the plugs from her ears. Other students yelled and separated down the rows in both directions.

Buddy looked down and saw the thin carpet through his shoes and the transparent crotch of his jeans. He glanced back at the frightened students.

"They can see me and hear me?"

He reached down and lifted the buds at the ends of the wires that attached to the impossible computer with a full color screen. Buddy placed them in his ears and heard music.

"I can touch things too."

He reached down and typed on the attached keyboard of the computer.

"Someone show me how this works. The world is depending on me, and I don't have much time."

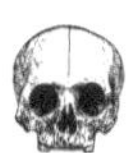

Buddy clutched his chest and opened his eyes to near darkness. "Am I dead?"

His voice did not echo.

Cammie touched his sweaty forehead, and he startled. She said, "We thought so. What were you thinking?"

Greg spoke from across the room. "Yeah, what were you thinking doing my little sister. We're friends."

Cammie shouted, "Shut up about it, Gregory."

"Keep it down. Every time you yell, the vamps find us. We're running out of places to hide."

Buddy cleared his throat. "Where are we?"

Greg looked around the room. "I don't know. Someone's house? I'm not sure the 'no inviting' thing works when we break into a place, and our house is burnt down thanks to you two taking a screw break."

Cammie shook her fists. "Shut up, Greg. I can date whoever I want."

Buddy stood and held the wall for balance. "Whoa, I never said we were dating, Cammie. Things were heated, we thought we were going to die, and you came on to me. I just kind of want to be free to see how things go, you know?"

Cammie stood and placed her hands on her hips. "But I gave you my cherry."

Greg covered his face and groaned. "Oh, God, who talks like that? I'm going to vomit."

Buddy shook his head. "No way you were a virgin."

Cammie shouted, "What?"

Greg stepped between his sister and Buddy.

He spoke as he held her away from clawing Buddy's throat out. "We'll kill him later. I promise. Why did you shock yourself back there, Buddy? What was that about?"

Buddy rubbed the sides of his head. "Both times that I almost died, I was projected forward into the future. It had to be twenty or thirty years—maybe more—but into the twenty-first century at least."

Greg let go of Cammie. "How's that possible?"

Cammie looked around Greg's shoulder. "Were there

flying cars?"

"I don't know. I was inside. But probably. That's not important. I was see-through like a ghost, but people could see me and hear me, and I could touch things."

Greg leaned forward. "Did you grab any future boobs?"

"Why would I do that, Greg? Why?"

"Future boobs might be totally awesome. We don't know unless we touch them."

Buddy shrugged. "They did all seem a lot bigger and firmer, now that you mention it."

Greg snapped his fingers. "I knew it."

"I hate you both." Cammie walked toward the door of the strange bedroom.

Buddy waved his hands. "Listen, in the future there's a program that everyone on the planet connects to through computers they carry with them all the time. Some of them are as small as a phone. They combine their brains all over the world and communicate instantly."

Cammie turned around beside the door. "They must be brilliant."

Buddy hummed and said, "Well, it was a lot of cat pictures and people arguing about dancing. I didn't understand most of it. The program is run by a powerful wizard that lives in a castle and slaughters his own animals."

"Do they not have a President anymore?" Greg asked.

"I couldn't tell for sure. I think so. Donald Trump was on there a lot. There was a lot from the guy that played the navigator on *Star Trek* and one of the *Golden Girls*. I think they become great philosophers in the future."

"Weird," Cammie said.

"Yeah." Buddy nodded. "The program has also created copies of famous people from the past that are long dead but gives quotes they never actually said."

"How does this help us now?" Greg asked.

Buddy steepled his hands in front of his face. "This may be bad. I think I saw one of the vampires in a video in the future. If I'm right, he becomes a federal agent and stays awake twenty-four hours a day torturing and killing people. Even the President has to do what he says. I think it was the President."

Greg sat down on the bed. "Then, we fail. They take over the world. Is it that Kip guy? I hate him the most."

Cammie spoke through her tears. "Can the wizard help?"

Buddy sighed. "I didn't find the answer this last time, but if we know the future, I think we can come back and change it. I was able to move stuff in the future. With the right knowledge, we might be able to move the present too."

Greg pointed. "What's that wrapped around your wrist?"

Buddy lifted his hand and unwound the black wires. He stared at the tiny earbuds at the ends.

"I brought something back with me."

"What are you saying?" Cammie asked.

"I can bring stuff back. If I find the right thing and the right knowledge about the vampires' weaknesses from the future, we can stop them."

Buddy pushed past Greg and took out his knife.

Greg followed. "What are you going to do?"

Buddy knelt down behind the stereo system, cutting the cords to the wall and holding them in a bundle.

Cammie said, "Buddy, don't do it. You'll kill yourself if you keep this up. I love you."

Buddy bowed his head. "Cammie, listen; you're great and all, but I'm not really looking for a heavy commitment at this point in my life. I'm sorry I gave you the wrong impression. I wasn't thinking clearly with all the vampires and my parents getting turned.

Things were crazy."

Greg grabbed Buddy's shoulder. "Let me do it, Buddy. You may not be able to take much more."

Buddy pushed Greg's hand away. "I have to do this. I've already been there twice. I know what to look for. I'm sorry I nailed your sister, man."

Greg nodded. "Yeah, I'm sorry too."

"I'm right here, you dorks," Cammie yelled.

Buddy touched his tongue to the exposed wires and jolted back in a rain of sparks.

Greg stomped out a flame that caught on the rug next to Buddy's body.

He looked up at his sister and said, "Should we do CPR again?"

Cammie crossed her arms. "I'm never touching him again."

The window shattered behind them, scattering glass across the room. Wind gusted through the room for no explicable reason. Greg hauled Buddy up onto his shoulder as he turned around.

Kip levitated outside the window, staring at them with his red eyes and mullet waving only in the back. He opened his mouth and revealed long fangs as he laughed.

Greg moaned. "God, Buddy is so heavy. I've carried him across town twice."

Cammie said, "We don't invite you in. Go away."

Kip threw back his head and laughed. "I don't need your invitation. You're in my house."

Cammie opened the door to the bedroom, and they ran.

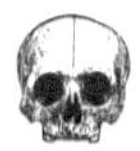

Buddy stood up and looked around a living room he

did not recognize. He held up his hands and looked through his fingers at a television that was long and flat like a movie screen. Still so weird to be see-through. He looked around the unoccupied room but did not see the projector.

Buddy cleared his transparent throat. His mouth tasted like charcoal.

He shoved magazines off the coffee table in front of the sofa. "I hope this works like a computer or a regular television."

Buddy lifted the remote in his ghost hands. He pushed the arrows and watched the square jump around the screen. He selected the red square and hoped for the best.

A series of movies scrolled by on the screen.

Buddy thumbed down the arrow to the word search and selected again. "I have no idea what I'm doing."

A screen appeared with a matrix of letters and numbers. Buddy smiled.

"Just like putting your name in the high score board on the games at the arcade. Some things never change. Thank God."

Buddy thumbed through quickly and typed in the word vampires. A selection of movies appeared, and he scrolled down the list.

"I need an answer."

He paused on one of the choices and hovered his ghostly thumb over the select button. He pressed and sat down on the couch.

As the movie played, he stared in terror and knew what he had to do.

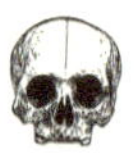

Buddy opened his eyes, staring up through the trees

at the night sky. "Where are we now?"

"The woods."

Cammie whispered. "You look dead, Buddy. Are you okay?"

Buddy sat up. "No, but I did what I had to do."

He spread his arms and levitated a few feet above the ground.

Greg broke a low branch off one of the trees and held it in front of him. "Run, Cammie."

Cammie didn't move. "They got you, Buddy?"

"I let it happen, but I am something different from them. I can stop them."

"You let it happen?" Greg said, "Why?"

Buddy sighed. "There are more terrifying vampires in the future. I can stop them now. They won't be expecting me."

Cammie whispered, "How do you feel?"

Buddy cast his eyes toward the ground. "Weary and melancholy."

"How can you stop them?" Greg asked.

Buddy turned his face up to the stars. "I can walk during the daylight."

"Great," Cammie said. "We'll wait until morning, and then we'll attack the other vampires. We can get that old, grizzly wise man that we ignored before the town was attacked to help us. We really owe him an apology."

"You don't want to see what happens to me in the sunlight. It's hideous."

Kip soared down through the leaves and hovered over the trio. Others followed from above, with only their red eyes showing.

Kip said, "Nice of you to join us, Buddy. I'll let you pick first, and we'll eat your leftovers."

"I have something more dramatic in mind," Buddy said.

He seized Kip's forearms, and they spun in the air for no reason. The pair crashed up through the trees as more of the vampires dove into the fight.

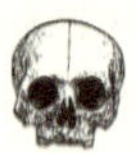

Cammie and Greg stepped over the bloody, burnt bodies that scattered the streets of the deserted town. Smoke rose up in the distance with no fire department to put out the blaze.

They stepped through the shattered door of the packing plant.

Cammie spotted Buddy in the corner, standing away from the light pouring through the windows.

She approached him. "It's finished, Buddy."

"You're sure?" he asked. "There's not one of them left?"

Greg shook his head as he stood behind his sister. "We looked everywhere. They're all gone. Even the grizzly old man said we beat them. He's giving us a ride to another town he assures us is vampire free. Are you coming?"

"I can't," Buddy said.

Cammie reached for Buddy, but he pulled away.

"You can go out in the daylight. I saw it. You will be like my own diamond earring."

Buddy shook his head. "I won't live like this. I won't sparkle in the sun and stalk young girls when I'm a hundred years old. You need to keep your promise to me."

He held out a sharpened chair leg.

Cammie shook her head. "I can't."

"You swore, Cammie. You swore it to me."

Greg nodded his head and turned to hide his tears. "I'll miss you, Buddy. Packing brats in a sausage factory will not be the same without you right behind me the whole time."

Buddy nodded. "Back at you."

Greg walked toward the broken door and covered his eyes.

Cammie said, "There has to be a way. Go back to the future and find another answer like you did before."

He shook his head. "You can't shock a heart that doesn't beat anymore."

"Yes, you can. That's exactly why they shock hearts, dummy."

"It's not what I meant, Cammie. It's a metaphor, sort of. Never mind. Just do this. Please."

Buddy shoved the stake into her hands.

Cammie leaned forward and kissed him on his cold mouth. "I love you, Buddy. I always will."

Buddy looked at his shoes. "Listen, I feel like I'm being clear here and you're just not getting it. What we did was fun, but you say the 'L' word way too easy. This is a lot of pressure for something that was just physical. Do you think you could just be cool about it?"

Cammie growled and drove the stake into Buddy's chest. Instead of bursting into flames like the others, he shriveled and slid down into a heap in the corner.

Cammie turned away and joined her brother by the door. "Are you okay, Greg?"

He nodded. "Yeah, I'm sorry he behaved like an ass after you guys did it."

She sighed. "He did save us, and I killed him like he asked. We'll call it even, I guess. Let's go outside and get some sun. I'm tired of being in the dark."

STILL

Eva awoke scared and confused in the dark every morning. Usually, she woke up cold and sweaty. Her tight braids often gave her a headache from trying to sleep inside the cramped, hard cabinet, but she didn't feel safe anywhere else anymore.

She stretched up one numb hand and felt for the latch inside the cabinet door. As she breathed in the stale air of the cramped space, Eva paused with her tingling fingers closed on the latch. She swallowed twice and forced herself to break the seal and swing open the doors.

Even through the dusty drapes, the brightness of morning burned her eyes. She pressed the heels of her hands to her sockets, making them wet with painful tears. With her eyes still covered, she folded out to her knees on the tile floor of the empty trophy room. Dust billowed up from her impact and stung her nose. She sneezed while still pressing her hands against her face.

She lowered her hands and looked across the film of neglect coating the tables and animal heads. It was her job to care for these things, but Eva had to keep the castle in a state of abandonment in order to survive.

She looked down at her own neglected clothes, with

holes and food stains across the front. Her brown arms and knees showed ashen through dead skin cells. Eva tried to remember her last bath. She needed to take one soon. As her grandmother had told it, thirteen-year-old girls needed to stay clean to stay healthy. Eva was glad the old woman had not lived to see this.

Eva considered a morning bath, but she feared being caught alone and naked, so she decided to put it off a while longer.

Her body shivered.

She took to her feet and walked out through the dining hall, into the corridor. Eva stretched her back until it popped three times. Putting her shoulder to the wall, she looked up at the sky through one of the open windows. Sunlight had broken through the cloud cover. It felt warm on her dark skin, but she did not allow herself to linger in plain sight.

Eva swallowed and looked down at the village below the castle and mountain. Purple crystals glinted from the sunlight striking the market place and atop broken wagons along the streets. She saw one purple crystalline statue leaning out an open window of one of the inns. Through the strange substance, Eva could see the woman's mouth had been open when she became stilled while hanging out that window.

"She was probably screaming when it happened."

She scanned the clouds to ascertain that none of the sky rafts were sailing across the blue between islands of white and grey. While she felt comforted that none of the deadly vessels were in sight, Eva knew they could drop in quickly and often did.

She cleared her throat and moved back into the shadows away from the windows. As she made her way down the stairs, she counted her steps to avoid being surprised and crying out when she came upon them.

Once she reached the corner leading into the kitchen, Eva paused and braced herself. She rounded the corner and stared into the purple-coated face of the kitchen mistress. In life, her skin had been a shade darker than Eva's and much darker than Eva's late grandmother. As Eva stared at the tower of crystals, the mistress of the kitchen appeared painted inside the giant jewel in shades of purple.

Eva always marveled that the kitchen servant managed to appear brave and resolved while everyone else seemed so afraid. She tried to imagine whether the woman had not had time to react or the creatures did not scare her.

"Nothing scared her," Eva said, "but she sure scared me."

She walked into the kitchen and counted seven more clusters of crystals. She was not sure why she always counted, but she did so every morning. Eva always played it out in her mind that the mistress was stilled in the hallway and then the invaders entered the kitchen. All seven faces inside showed fear. A few lifted knives or dough rollers as weapons but held them clutched in their purple shells unused.

Eva continued through the kitchen. She paused and lifted a piece of hardtack from one of the bins. The supply grew low, and she would have to venture outside soon.

"I'll put it off just a while longer."

As she ate, Eva stepped into the darkness of the service stairs. With the dryness of the hardtack and the silent blackness around her, Eva found it hard to swallow. She continued up the stairs, counting steps.

At thirty steps, she paused and reached out with her free hand. She felt the tacky surface of the purple crystals she could not see. They formed around what she always assumed was one of the knights guarding the stairs or coming down to investigate the noise in the kitchen. She guessed that the jagged protrusion in front of him was his encased sword.

Eva counted steps until she reached the door and cracked it onto the narrow passage inside the wall of the throne room. Closed panels led out to the right of the passage, but light came from the open arch all the way at the end on the left.

Even though she knew it to be clear, she counted her steps anyway.

She paused at the archway and looked down at the flagstones at her feet. Eva shivered as she stared at the purple stain that had spread from the throne dais to the back wall of the room. Her assessment was that the knight might have killed one before he took the stairs, but that didn't seem to fit. Maybe her own prince took one before he became still himself. He had saved her, which was more than any of the others had accomplished, even though the prince was just fifteen.

Eva stepped around the unhuman blood from a body that had been removed by the strange attackers.

"It means that you do bleed."

Eva crossed the throne room, chewing her flavorless bread and dropping crumbs like she would have never done months earlier, before the sky rafts fell on their kingdom the first time.

She set her breakfast on the ledge by the main entrance and lifted the hammer and chisel she had left there the day before.

Eva turned and counted the figures in the room, from the king slumped in purple crystals on his throne to the queen spilled across the stairs in a most unseemly way to all the still attendants. She came up with thirteen and she stopped. Eva turned in a full circle. She counted again and then a third time. She still counted thirteen purple forms instead of fourteen like every day before that.

Eva heard the click and hiss echo in from the main corridor. She clutched the hammer and chisel to her chest and ran for the dark service entrance near the stain of purple blood. She ran across the room but heard something thump inside the wall.

"I'm trapped."

Eva slid under one of the tables and curled into a ball.

"You can't hide from monsters under tables."

She bit her lip as she saw their grey feet and grotesque, slender legs lead into the throne room through the main entrance. In the stories of her grandmother, trolls were large and fat. The trolls from out of the stars were ugly in their leanness of body and their oversized, hairless skulls. Somehow, their fat heads and wide, ebony eyes made them seem smarter and more dangerous. All Eva could think was that if she could stab them, they would bleed out purple.

She counted five sets of star troll legs.

They paced around the room to each of the clusters of purple crystals. She could not see it, but she heard the siren's whistle from one of their bejeweled armlets. In their last three returns to inspect their work, they had circled the castle, letting their armlets sing to each of the stilled humans. She had managed to flit about, staying a step ahead of them until they left again. At this moment, she was pinned in and hiding under a table.

The troll feet stopped and turned toward her. The tone of the armlet's song changed. Eva cringed as they clicked and hissed at one another.

As they approached the table together, Eva backed out from under it and bumped into the crystals of the jester stilled in mid weeping.

Eva slid around and crouched between him and the wall.

Through the filter of the purple crystals around the jester's legs, she saw the bulbous heads and eyes of the star trolls leaning over the table and staring as one of them pointed his screaming armlet. Under the terrible whistle, she heard them clicking and hissing at each other.

A purple beam of magic sprayed from the armlet into the jester's chest. The light wrapped around and sparked in front of Eva's face. She pressed the back of her head to the wall as the crystals crackled and expanded. Eva closed her eyes and prepared to be stilled.

The beam stopped, and the armlet changed tone slightly. The trolls clicked and hissed.

Eva opened her eyes and saw the sharp points of the new crystals inches from her face. She took slow breaths to avoid being heard. As the trolls moved toward the entrance to the throne room, she felt the heat off the jester's back and smelled the odor that reminded her of boiling urine.

The trolls stopped at the door and began clicking and hissing more frantically.

Eva tried to move her hands but couldn't. She panicked and imagined herself starving to death, trapped and half-stilled. As she glanced down, she let go of the hammer and chisel, realizing her hands were free but the tools had been partially encased.

She slid her body out from behind the twice stilled jester and peered around his side. The trolls gathered at the ledge next to the door and tittered at each other like angry insects. One of them poked with one long finger. Eva saw her partially eaten hardtack resting on the ledge in front of the trolls, and she shook her head.

The hand closed over her mouth from behind and pulled her down to the floor. She inhaled through her nostrils, but her breath caught when she stared up into the eyes of her prince.

He whispered, "I just followed your trail up into the service stairs behind the wall. Why did you leave the cabinet, Eva?"

Eva saw the crust of purple residue over his skin and clothes.

She pulled his hand away. "It has been months, Roland."

The fifteen-year-old boy glanced around the room, looking younger and more afraid than Eva ever remembered seeing him in her years in the castle's service.

"How many months?"

"Almost two full seasons."

Roland shook his head, dropping purple crumbs from his blond hair. "They have been here this whole time?"

Eva sat up. "They return to look. I've been chiseling you out of their terrible purple cocoon every day since they stilled you."

He leaned forward and kissed her hard on the lips. His mouth felt chapped, and his breath tasted like rotten meat, but she kissed him back in joy, placing her hand on his crusty cheek.

The troll's clicking and their singing armlet crossed the throne room again, and the couple separated. They lowered to the floor behind the table.

Eva pointed to the service entrance, and they crawled along the wall toward the blood-stained back corner. As the trolls stepped past the end of the table, the couple rounded the corner.

They paused in silence. The trolls clicked and hissed louder.

In the low light, Eva and Roland exchanged a look. They leaned out to see around the doorway.

The trolls stood around the broken residue of the crystals where Prince Roland had been stilled for the past two seasons.

Eva took his hand and led him back down the stairs. As she counted, she steered him past the frozen knight and out through the kitchen. When she turned the opposite way from the kitchen mistress, Roland pulled Eva up short.

"We should go back to the cabinet. You were safe there."

"Not all problems can be solved by hiding in a cabinet, Roland."

The clicking and hissing picked up from inside the kitchen. One of the bins overturned with a crash.

The couple ran down the hall and cut down a spiral stair leading into the belly of the castle. Eva took Roland to the right, down the corridor at the bottom, and through an empty stable, to a door looking out on a sloped field leading down the mountain, away from the village.

Roland held out his hand as they reached the door. "Wait. Let's be sure our path is clear before we flee."

"I'm not sure how much time we have before they track us."

He licked his dry lips. "Why didn't you flee sooner if they kept returning?"

"They did not know I was here before," she said. "Now they have seen my breakfast and found your broken shell. There are probably more coming."

Roland sighed and shook his head. "I wish you had fled sooner, Eva."

Eva put a hand to his cheek, thinking about seeing him day after day stilled inside the star trolls' crystals. "I don't know how to escape monsters that drop out of the sky, and I could not leave you."

He nodded. "Then we will figure it out together and maybe someday return to reclaim what is ours."

"Ours?" Eva laughed. "Would your father approve?"

"Right now, we are a kingdom of two, so what does it matter?"

Eva leaned out and said, "I think it is as clear as we can expect. We still may not make it far."

"Let's try."

Eva swallowed. "First, tell me, was it you that spilled the star troll blood in the throne room?"

Roland turned his eyes to the ground. "My family was sealed in when I returned. I did slay one, leaving my sword in him, and then succumbed to their magic. I crumbled to the floor this morning and thought no time had passed. I came to your cabinet and tracked you back around. I'll need a new sword."

Eva turned his face. "Or more chisels and hammers."

She kissed his chapped lips and took his hand. The hisses and clicks echoed up the corridor behind the stable.

Without another word, they ran out into the light together.

SEERSUCKER MOTHERFUCKER

Sally Finch fired a .45 slug through the plate glass parlor window of the Harper estate at the face of Kelly Harper. Kelly would have ducked had she not been staring dumbfounded at the gold-plated revolver Sabastian Finch had accepted in Christian charity and Southern hospitality from Castro over cigars. Sally clutched the golden gun, hammer cocked. She stood below the porch, aiming through the railing pickets with legs spread and steady in hiking boots under her ivory Sunday dress.

Her aim was true.

Kelly had just knelt on the sofa when she spotted Sally pointing murder from between the slats of the porch. Kelly was flushed before she knew someone intended her dead. The blush had risen on her chest above the line of her pink dress.

She had already been smitten by Coop Bainbridge, who was on the other end of the sofa from her, having stopped in for a visit after Sunday supper.

Kelly paused too long with one knee up on the sofa cushion, like a harlot posing for a broke painter down by the docks. Far too long in that position for Aunt Areene on the admiral's chair next to the fireplace, which was venting summer heat. Areene could see her niece's indiscretion under Coop's leering eyes but not the golden Communist revolver that froze Kelly in place perched beside the plate glass.

"Kelly, settle your—"

The report of the revolver vibrated the wall with cannon force. The frame held, but the slug burst through a tapered hole three times its width. Seven cracks radiated in smooth curves out from the hole but not as far as the oak panels surrounding the window.

Centered on Kelly's face.

Coop jolted at the noise, Aunt Areene thought as she choked on her scolding words. Coop thought to turn his head to see Kelly's position on the sofa better, but the muscles did not respond to the final thought before the bullet, intended and perfectly aimed at Kelly, deflected hard and punched through the back of Coop's skull.

It was Coop's fault; after all, he had not been the intended of that bullet. Maybe the next one would have been marked for him, had Kelly gotten her due for being the object of Coop Bainbridge's affections after he broke off courtship with Sally. This, like many things about that sultry Sunday afternoon, would be unknowable, as Sally never took a second shot with her father's gun.

She turned and stepped on one of the hydrangeas as she fled the scene—across the lawn toward the street and the alley between the Methodist church and the florist. She tripped on the hem of her dress and slid on her knees, staining her Sunday best green under the massive limbs of the live oak draped in Spanish moss.

Kelly stared after her in shock.

Coop folded forward into his own lap and toppled over into the floor, bleeding into the thick oriental rug. His blood turned the elaborate blue and purple patterns into a wash of blackness.

Aunt Areene screamed until Ratcliff Harper and his son, Norton, ran in from the dining room. She took a breath, and they both looked at her. Ratcliff held a hunting rifle, Norton a shotgun. Areene resumed screaming.

Coop's brains and three of his teeth were sprayed across the marble top of the coffee table. Bits of skin from his nose or cheek stuck to the cover of the family Bible. A sharp triangle of skull bone oozed down the gilded edges of the pages on a small glob of blood and brain. A burst eyeball sat in a jelly puddle atop the music box, with a few inches of optic nerve trailing behind.

Norton coughed and asked his sister, "What happened?"

Kelly pointed at the bullet hole bending the light from outside into swirls of white and shadow. "Finch."

"That bastard bean farmer Sabastian shooting at my daughter on Sunday?" Ratcliff raised his rifle and stepped over Coop's body toward the front door.

"No, Sally Finch. She shot at Coop." Kelly knew it wasn't true, and she hated Sally as much as the Devil, but she lied to her father anyway. Something about letting him know she was the target made her more afraid than the memory of staring down the barrel of gold and death.

Ratcliff paused and glanced down at the dead Bainbridge boy fouling their carpet, then he burst through the front door, onto the porch. Norton followed.

Under the oak, Sally Finch stood squared, aiming that shiny pistol at Carson Harper, the middle child. He held his hands raised, with his bird rifle gripped at the stock in his right fist.

Norton pushed past his father and yelled to his brother, "Carson."

Sally turned and aimed on the porch. "I'll kill you all.

Let me go."

Carson dropped his arms and let the barrel of his rifle fall across his left forearm, trained on Sally. He slid his finger inside the trigger guard.

Ratcliff raised a hand off his rifle. "No!"

Carson fired, and his shot tore through Sally's neck. Blood spewed out in arcs from the arteries on both sides. Her throat wrinkled like she'd turned eighty in an instant. Her head lolled forward, and she dropped to her grassy knees. She teetered for a moment as her dress dyed red from the top down, then fell to her back, her legs pinned under her, her father's gun lying inches from her hand in the mud between the thick roots of the great tree.

Ratcliff and Norton charged down the steps and across the lawn.

The pastor stepped out of the Methodist church. Others filtered out of diners and cafeterias up the street. A sedan whined to a halt on thin brake pads as the woman leaned out the passenger window, holding her hat and squinting.

Sally choked on her blood and clawed at the mud shy of the pistol's butt. Her eyes rolled up in her head as Ratcliff Harper and his sons stood over her.

Kelly stepped between them and lifted the revolver from the ground. She thumbed back the hammer.

Ratcliff scanned the streets, looking at all the townspeople watching. "Kelly, don't."

"He never liked you, you dirty bitch." She fired through Sally's forehead, causing her head to bounce, and stilled the girl's gagging.

The sedan raced away, and the minister slammed himself inside the sanctuary. Other families ran to their cars and pulled away from the curb, no doubt to be the first to tell Sabastian Finch how the Harpers murdered his daughter in cold blood.

Ratcliff pried the gun out of Kelly's hand and held it out to Carson. "You take this over to the church. Bang on the doors until that limp-wristed preacher opens them. Give him this and tell him we are bringing the bodies of Sally Finch and Cooper Bainbridge to lie in state. Sally murdered Coop out of jealousy and then drew down on us, forcing us to defend ourselves. Go."

Carson took the revolver, and Ratcliff took his bird rifle, holding a rifle in each fist. Carson ran. More of the townspeople scattered when they saw him coming.

"Norton, go get everyone. All your uncles, cousins—everyone! All Harpers need to be locked down here and ready for war before the Finches know what happened. Don't stop for anyone. Run them over if you have to. Don't let yourself get stopped and ambushed. Every man, woman, and child from our family needs to be here before the Finches hunt them all down for revenge. Go."

Norton, still holding his shotgun, ran for the truck, which was parked in the detached garage leading to the backstreet off the end of the property.

"Kelly." Ratcliff had to turn her away from Sally's body and lift her chin for her to look at him. "Get your grandpa and tell him we need help wrapping these bodies and getting them over to the church before everyone gets to town. Move your ass, girl."

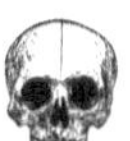

The pastor backed his chair as far as he could into the marble table behind his desk and leather rolling chair. The glassware hidden in the cabinets below jingled. The bottles behind the secret compartment were getting low. He could tell just from the tone.

The Methodist minister didn't know what to do with

his hands. He kept folding and unfolding them over the top of his lap in a compulsive pattern he feared might resemble masturbation.

Sabastian Finch sat across from the pastor, his white hair coiffed high and sweeping in the front into magnificent waves through the rest of his locks—too deliberate to be accidental or easy. The minister tried to imagine the man getting ready after hearing his daughter had been murdered. He could have dressed before church, but the pastor had not seen Sabastian, nor the rest of the Finches, during either morning service. He could not bear the thought that Master Finch had moved his membership and his tithe to another congregation. If it was the Baptists, then the minister's days were surely numbered.

The bushy handlebars of Sabastian's mustache cascaded down to a sharp triangle of beard oiled to a sure point. He wore a string black tie, which hung wilted and long under his chin. His pleated suit alternated green and white over the seersucker summer material of his jacket and pants where he sat with his legs crossed in the minister's study.

The suit and white shirt were hardly the dress of a man seeking violent solutions. His folded legs and posture in the chair spoke of calm control too.

But ...

But if rumors were to be believed, then the man had killed for far less, and there was no imagining that he would be satisfied with less than cutting off a generation and salting the earth over all the Harper property.

The minister feared his blood might begin the fertilization to cry out from the ground to God and these angry Southern devils.

The golden gun sat on the pastor's desk between the inkwell and his Bible, the butt turned in invitation to Finch's grasp and the barrel pointed at the pastor's chest in threat.

"I simply opened the doors of the church to accept the bodies out of respect to the losses of both the Finches and the Bainbridges," the minster answered finally. "I had no intention of speaking for or negotiating on behalf of the Harpers in this matter. I sent word to you as soon as I heard, without delay."

"If you don't speak for him," Sabastian steepled his fingers, "then why do you petition for his life to my face?"

The minster swallowed and shook his head rapidly in tight fractions of motion. "No. That's not what I meant, sir. I'm sorry. I simply meant that there might be a course for peace."

"You should be advocating for me." Sabastian leaned forward and uncrossed his legs. "The Harpers aren't even Methodist, for God's sake. This is the moment you should be pulling out verses on brimstone and Psalms about bleeding out our enemies to sacrifice to the God of the Old Testament. You got one of those sermons to share for me and the killers of my daughter?"

"I called you as soon as I heard."

Sabastian gritted his teeth and snatched up his revolver from the desktop to train on the pastor's voice box. "You should have had enough tallywacker between your legs to use this thing on Harper, either to hold him until I got here or put one in his knee to be sure he couldn't crawl back into his hole. You care about lives? Then you should know that making me go into his house after him will cost the most. Maybe it's only your life which matters to you, and my girl is just a sack of meat bleeding down the carved legs of your altar."

The minster raised his hands and quivered in his chair, as if developing palsy or the shakes from too long without a nip. "I did not think it my place to decide these things for you, sir. Not my place to use another man's gun."

Sabastian leaned his elbows on the edge of the desk and kept his aim. "Inaction is a decision, and sometimes a sin too."

"I had no part in this drama or its consequences. It was done by the time I knew anything." The minister swallowed and blinked rapidly with his hands still raised. "Where did your daughter get your prized firearm in the first place, and what was her intent in bringing it to the Harper property? That is the more important question, I think."

Sabastian's eyes widened, and his nostrils flared. He raised one eyebrow and opened the golden cylinder to see it empty. He set the empty gun on the table with the firing cylinder still opened out. He reached under the thin material of his jacket and drew an ordinary black pistol from a holster under his arm, thumbed the hammer back, and aimed again.

The minister coughed and held his arms straight out in front of him with palms open and fingers splayed. "No. No. No. Don't. Please. This isn't my doing. I meant no offense and have no part in this. Please, sir."

Sabastian shook his head. "Shameful display from a man who believes Heaven awaits. I wondered where your ugly boldness surfaced from. I suppose one unloaded gun is the trick to help a coward find his tongue."

"I'm sorry."

"Give me the bullets you took from my gun."

The minster shook as he pulled out the desk drawer above his lap. He took out four bullets. They rattled in his fist as he extended his hand.

"Put them back where you found them, preacher."

The minsters fingered them blind into the slots of the open chambers. He left two empty chambers, but not next to each other.

"You smeared the gold with your flop sweat. Clean it."

The minister looked around but then used the sleeve of his dark coat to wipe off the back of the chambers.

Sabastian stared a moment longer before he eased the hammer down and holstered the dark weapon under his arm again. He pressed the gold cylinder back into the body of the gun and lifted the Castro revolver in his fist and down by his side.

He left through the office door directly into the sanctuary without another word and without closing the door.

Finches stood from the pews near the front, facing the two bodies wrapped in bloody linen. Others stood straight from where they leaned below stained-glass windows.

Sabastian's brother, Mace Finch, pushed past his son Cody as he stepped into the center aisle. Uncle Howard, Cousin Spencer, and Zachariah closed in around the sides. Each had guns holstered, with long guns over their shoulders or strapped to their backs. Aunt Elizabeth and Susannah stood strapped and ready as well. Sabastian saw eyes rimmed red all around, but he read rage in them and not sorrow.

"What do we know?" Sabastian asked.

Mace stepped forward and rolled his rifle from his shoulder to the carpet like a cane. "Your sons are outside with the others, surrounding the estate from cover. No one is coming in or out. There are a couple in the garage too. We have dry brush and matches ready to smoke them out once the business starts."

"Do we got enough to do what needs doing?"

"Brother, we are fighters all." He lifted his rifle and clutched it across his chest. "Neighbors stepping up too. Even that fellow Smith and his boy stepped up and took position."

"Smith?" Sabastian narrowed his eyes. "The Chinaman?"

Cody said, "Think he's Laotian."

Mace cut a look at his son, and Sabastian shook his head. "What the hell is Laotian? Is that like elves?"

"It's like a Chinaman," Mace said, "but not from China."

"He runs the China Noodle House, right?"

Mace nodded. "His son is half American. They attend the foreigner service here on Sunday afternoons. That makes them kind of American and mostly Methodist."

"The noodles are good too," Cody said.

"Damn it, boy." Mace gritted his teeth and then took a deep breath. "They brought their own guns and are ready to fight to avenge Sally."

Sabastian faced the altar. The Bainbridge boy's hand had slipped out of his linen shroud and folded open near the bloody wrappings of his daughter, as if awaiting her to join fingers with him. He felt an insane desire to shoot the dead boy's hand for the impropriety of it all.

Blood coated the contours of his daughter's shroud in abstract patterns. The red spots floated in his vision and made him dizzy. Soon, all he could see were the clouds of red bleeding across his vision.

He wanted to mourn her, to touch her, to hold her, to bury her, but he wanted blood spilled in her name until it flowed through the streets of the town like an Aztec slaughter. His rage required an extinction level event to quench.

He would not touch her mangled body nor attempt to wash it clean until he could offer up that much and nothing less under the eyes of God, who must surely be as hungry for blood as Sabastian felt. If not, He could be no true God at all.

Sabastian tried to blink the red out of his vision but failed. He said, "Good enough. Nobody shoot any Chinamen today. We're all fighting for the Finch name now."

Mace clapped a hand on his brother's shoulder as they walked up the aisle toward the back of the sanctuary and the front of the building. The others fell in step behind.

Mace said, "That's real Christian of you, Brother. Mom would be proud."

Sabastian shook his head. "Not sure how she would feel about murder on a Sunday. Of course, as I recall, she passed on a Saturday night, so it ain't so much her place to say anymore."

They burst through the church doors into the sunlight.

The minister, in his office, poured himself a tumbler full to the rim with hot brown liquid without bothering to close the secret compartment back.

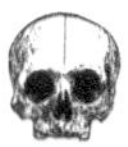

Ratcliff examined the silk tie but then pulled the knot free and tossed it aside. He left the peach shirt open at the collar under his light blue seersucker. Good breathing fabric for combat in the sultry summer air.

"What kind of sack of shit would wear a tie to a gun battle anyhow?" he asked the mirror and then turned away.

He smoothed down his dark hair and then took up his guns, one at a time, off the bed to check the loads before holstering them about his body. He took up two rifles with no intention of manning both, but there were a lot of extended family packed downstairs and around the windows.

"Always good to have backups."

Ratcliff Harper took the stairs two at a time. Dr. Hess met him at the bottom of the stairs and accepted one of the rifles. "They got us locked down, just like you said they would."

Ratcliff patted the doctor's shoulder. "We brought in everyone we could. It'll have to do."

"Maybe you can still talk him down."

Ratcliff took a deep breath. "Maybe you should get ready to be busy today, Doc."

He passed the parlor and heard Aunt Areene loading up there. It sounded like belt load ammo, but he wasn't certain and didn't look.

He passed Grandpa, from his late wife's side of the family, in a rocker at a window with an open sash in the hallway. The old man had a shotgun across his lap as he worked the rocker. Ratcliff patted the old man's shoulder, and the old-timer nodded. That was all the exchange they usually shared most Sundays.

In the kitchen, Norton sat with his arms curled around his plate, his guns laid out on both sides of him. He sopped up the greenish-brown gravy from the butterbeans with a square of mill cornbread. He hunched over the food in a way that reminded Ratcliff of the former prisoners he hired for the fields.

"You not get enough at supper, boy? Getting ready to run and shoot makes you want to have a full belly?"

Norton tilted back his mason jar of sweet tea before he answered. "Just didn't know when I was going to get a chance to eat again."

"Wrap it up and see if we can get some good people out in the shrubbery without getting picked off. More behind the cover of the retaining walls too. I'd rather not start this thing already at our last stand and count on those dummies in the garage to save us. Such things don't typically end well. If we could get any of them in a crossfire instead of us, that would be much preferred as well."

Norton stood and ate the whole way taking his plate to the sink. Ratcliff stared down at his son's guns, framing the empty setting at the table. He chewed at his lip and turned away to head for the front door.

Carson squatted low and peered over the edge of the tall, narrow glass beside the door.

"What is it?" Ratcliff stood flank to his son.

"They just exited the church and are taking up with men already in position. They're on the streets behind cars and barricades. Up in the windows and on roofs of the buildings on the cross streets near every intersection."

"Where's Kelly?"

"Upstairs window behind the oak tabletop."

Ratcliff took hold of the door latch and rested his rifle across his neck behind his head.

"You sure that's a good idea, Daddy?"

Ratcliff closed his eyes slowly and opened them again. "I'm sure it is not, but I should go on record as having tried before everyone ends up dead today."

He opened the door, stepped out on the porch, and stopped at the top of the steps.

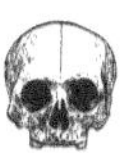

After Sabastian slammed through the church doors with Mace, it took three full seconds for his eyes to adjust. As he felt his way blind down the cast iron railing, he imagined a Harper kid breaking protocol and popping him in the chest while he was vulnerable. It would start everything, but the Finches would begin at a disadvantage. Maybe the kids would be smarter and more ruthless about these things. Possibly such a terror would avoid so much killing in the first place.

But you can't have a second generation when daughters are laid down in cold blood.

He saw the Harper house first as his vision returned. Eyes and faces peered from shadows and corners in every window. He wanted to personally put a bullet into each one.

The contingent from the church spread out in both directions on the street to take places with their fellows behind vehicles at various firing points.

Sabastian sidled down beside Newton behind the door of a Chrysler. Newt aimed over the hood at the Harper porch.

"Where are your brothers?"

"Boone is around back. He sent word that a few Harper cousins are moving out behind the retaining walls. He says he has a bead on them, the backdoor, and the garage, and they'll light 'em up, making them wish they'd stayed inside. Foster is prone in a drainage ditch, crawled up into the ivy. He's alone but has a good cross on the front, the side yard, and the second floor. If he gets in trouble, he can drop back to the cars in front of the florist for cover."

"How many?"

"A few dozen, all told. Can't be sure. More drove up on Miller and on Third since we been here. They turned tail and left when they saw how things were. I took it on myself to have a few guys follow them. They aren't to do anything but find where they hide and come back. We can pick them off later, if it gets to that."

"Good. I'm going to work my way around to one of the other positions, I think."

Newton said, "Me and the others are a might hot about not getting to see Sally."

Sabastian shook his head and rose up to peer over the hood with his son. "You wouldn't have wanted to see it. It was … Not yet. We'll deal with this first, and then that."

Newton looked at his father, then turned his attention back on the Harper house.

Sabastian scanned the street to the other vehicle firing zones and shooters on the surrounding roofs. Mr. Smith from the Noodle House and his half-American son were over and behind the next pickup truck down the block. Smith cut a look at Sabastian. He nodded, and Sabastian nodded back.

The front door swung open with a creak, and fingers tensed around triggers. A few more knuckles slipped into trigger guards.

Ratcliff Harper, in light blue linen, strolled out onto the porch with his rifle rested behind his head. Other than strapping at every ankle, hip, armpit, and other joints, he appeared to be strolling out for fresh air and an afternoon walk.

He stopped at the top of the steps and called, "Sabastian, we need to talk—parlay—before anyone else is lost in tragedy. I know blood has been spilt and retribution is surely inevitable at this point, but I still owe you an explanation and an honest exchange before more bullets fly. Will you meet me halfway to let me tell you what happened before we fall back to our positions of war this afternoon?"

Sabastian stood up behind the car.

Newton whispered, "Daddy. Don't."

"Not sure how you intend to talk me down from love and anger for my daughter, Harper."

Ratcliff shook his head, rubbing the base of his skull against the barrel of his rifle rested there. "Wouldn't dream of it. Wouldn't disrespect you by even trying. I want to let you know how the Bainbridge boy became the deadly pawn in the middle of this nightmare. You deserve to know that much before this thing begins."

"The preacher already relayed your excuses to me

when you tried to get him to bargain for your skin."

"Not sure I trust a Methodist preacher to properly explain sin, blood, and sacrifice. They are more the 'Sweet By And By' kind. You and I speak the language of violence and death more fluently, so it should be us that share the details of this unfortunate afternoon. Will you meet me at the tree for a conference, sir? We can speak, stay our guns, and then move back in position for whatever must come next."

Sabastian stepped out from around the nose of the car and placed one foot on Harper grass. Ratcliff took the next step down.

"She killed Coop," the girl shouted through the upstairs window.

Ratcliff whipped his head up to look skyward from under the porch cover. "Kelly, shut up and stay down."

Sabastian brought the golden gun up. The Finch family and friends lifted their aim as well.

Kelly's voice echoed into the streets of the town. "Sally fired through the plate glass right at us and killed Coop because she was jealous. She did it with that ridiculous gun you're holding right now."

Ratcliff rolled the rifle off his neck and swung it down in his grasp to aim on the porch steps. "Shut up, girl."

She persisted. "She threatened my brother, Carson, and then pointed it at us again. He shot her, but hit her in the throat. As she choked on her own blood, I took the gun from her and finished her off. That's how they both ended up dead. It was her doing."

"Kelly, damn it." Ratcliff met Finch's eyes in a wild gaze across the lawn.

Sabastian drew his mouth into a tight line before he said, "Send out Carson and Kelly to answer to us, and we'll start there. Maybe have a trial. We have a good tree out front of the courthouse and cells underneath, however that plays out."

"The judge is your second cousin," Ratcliff said. "It's like she says—Sally came here with your gun to start unprovoked violence. No need to drag us all down."

Foster rose up out of the drainage ditch near the ivy. "Fuck you, Harper."

Ratcliff trained the rifle on the ditch. Sabastian lowered his aim from the upstairs window to the porch.

A shot cracked off. It echoed, and the noise died without anyone reacting at first. Neither Ratcliff, Sabastian, nor Foster was missing a bullet. So small. It could have been around back or even down the street. Nothing loud enough to match any of the weapons in sight. Maybe a .22, by the unimpressive report.

Finch's people looked around for confirmation or instruction.

Sabastian and Ratcliff met eyes again, both wide and desperate. Ratcliff opened his palms, still clutching the rifle with one thumb. He lowered his weapon slowly. Sabastian slid his finger out of the trigger guard.

Three shots cracked off from the cars and two from the side windows in a barrage that prevented anyone from judging who shot second. Louder weapons with higher calibers than the first mystery shot. One was a shotgun from a hallway window, even though it was likely out of range of the street.

Foster then fired twice from his knees in the ditch, tearing siding off the house next to Ratcliff. Ratcliff Harper slapped his hand to his face and scrambled over the porch through the open door.

Sabastian fired once into the house through the door, hoping he hit someone or something Ratcliff loved. The next chamber clicked empty.

A tall window shattered next to the door, and someone fired from there.

Sabastian backed off the grass into the street.

Smoke erupted from both directions. Windows on

the cars and the house shattered. Dark holes opened in wood and metal. Sabastian wondered if everyone had parked with gas tanks facing away from the house as instructed. He also wished Newt hadn't sent anyone away to track Harper cowards.

Newton's gun erupted over the hood several times, and then he stopped to reload.

The front door slammed, and Sabastian fired another shot through the wood face. He raised his aim carefully between branches and fired twice through the upstairs window at the girl's voice. Someone screamed, and dark wood splintered out of the opening. Too dark to be part of the house. Must have been furniture inside.

The golden gun clicked empty three times, and Sabastian set it on the hood as he drew another, less flashy weapon. The windshield beside him shattered inward.

Newt grabbed and wrinkled the material of his father's jacket. "Get down, sir."

Sabastian knelt behind the cover of the car with his son.

The ivy next to Foster ripped apart, exposing ugly brown runners underneath and a rich smell of clipped greenery. He turned in the ditch and ran for the cover of the cars. He stood straight and arched his back as he clutched a hand over his shirt at kidney level. Blood sprayed into the air from his shoulder and drifted off and down on the breeze.

Foster dropped his gun in the ditch.

"Son of a bitch," Sabastian breathed.

Foster's body jarred three times, and he fell to his knees. His head folded open in the back and one eye vanished into a dark, bloody hole. He pitched forward to his face.

Newt stopped to reload again.

Mace dropped to his belly and fired into the bushes

at the side of the house. Two Harpers rolled back from cover and slid down the grimy bricks at the base of the house, slumped dead behind the shrubbery.

The parlor window cracked as bullets bounced off the thick glass at angles. One struck the corner, blasting wood and pasting the glass white with cracks from one end to the other. Sabastian squared and fired through the center of the window not three inches to the left of the bullet hole left by his late daughter. The window exploded inward, and more Finches fired through the opening.

Metal gears cranked and clanged. A massive silver Gatlin gun rolled into position and then dropped its heavy shaft horizontal, with its spiral of barrels aimed out.

The machine spun and boomed with each bold shot, one after the other. The old woman pivoting the weapon to and fro wore black goggles as she unleashed hell and metal. The shots skimmed furrows through the Harpers' lush grass, exposing ugly clay. Tires flattened on the cars as the bullets bounced up from the curb.

She raised the weapon's nose from the groundward aim and sheered the top off of the car beside Sabastian's position. Mr. Smith and the white men scattered along the street for better cover.

Brick exploded off the building faces across the street. Pipes were exposed, ruptured, and then sprayed water or steam out into the hail of bullets. Shots sparked off the copper gutters, caving them in and screaming away the green grime down to the beautiful metal in angry slashes. The Finch snipers rolled away from the edges of attack and slithered on their bellies over the roof gravel.

The old, deadly bitch swung the weapon back as small hands below the window line fed another belt into the macabre contraption.

The church bell barked out an unholy ring as the steeple was chewed apart along its base. The whole spire with the cross on top plummeted straight down through the sanctuary ceiling and took out three respected families' pews right in the middle. The pastor watched from the open door of his office as he refilled his tumbler. He lowered himself carefully, so as not to spill any, and hid below his desk.

The Gatlin Dragon continued to breathe death outside. Bark erupted off the century old branches hanging low and majestic over the lawn. Spanish moss dropped to the ground and covered the bloody patch left by Sally's death. White pulp unraveled after the dark armor of the live oak bark ripped away. The line of fire tore across the trunk, and massive branches gave up the ghost as they crashed to the ground with a ton of authority felt all the way to the river.

The snipers on the roof rose behind pipe chimneys, and men on the ground outside the line rose to concentrate fire through the windows. Books on the parlor shelves vomited pages out of their spines. Fire from ricochets rebounded off the oven-hot tubes of the spinning barrels of the Gatlin. She continued to sweep fire.

The Harpers in the upper rooms took practiced shots down on the distracted Finches. A few good cousins fell injured or dead, but they pressed the attack in dogging the aunt and her great horror of a gun.

After the tree lost much of its glory, the florist's shop blew apart from the front. Petals of Easter colors and brighter hues of lust plumed into the air and rained down onto the street—and Sabastian's shoulders—like a grand celebration of Sunday fireworks.

Sabastian rose and took aim through the clear lines left by the trimmed tree. He fired once, and the old aunt staggered back, holding her chest. The light fire, which remained from the other windows, seemed small and weak in comparison to moments before. The Finch fire continued until a bolt popped loose and the gun collapsed in on itself. A young boy rose with a fresh belt of ammo but nowhere to put it. He took a stray shot between the goggle lenses and fell.

The Finches reloaded and took shots through the remaining windows.

Sabastian looked for a target but found no one manning the windows across the front. The battle continued along the side and back for now.

Sabastian smiled. "Newt, gather everybody left alive on this side, and let's charge these godless bastards."

The gunfire returned to the front lawn as Sabastian Finch led the charge. A couple were winged and dropped to the scarred grass in surprise. Others dove and curled into balls behind the felled oak branches. Sabastian noted the cowards for later. He and Newt—and most of the rest, including the ladyfolk, praise God—leapt the branches and skirted the light fire to trample into the cover of the porch.

Sabastian kept aim on the open front parlor for any Harper bastard to show his greasy face, but none took the position. He looked his son in the face with pride, and without a word, they kicked the Harper front door above the latch together, caving the thing in with splinters and broken metal.

The Finches invaded. Cousins rushed the kitchen and opened fire. One took the stairs, then took a bullet center mass and tumbled back down in a heap. Others made for cover outside the door and returned fire.

Sabastian and Newt sidestepped away from the banister and deeper into the house. A couple boys, Mace's nephews by marriage, pounced on the aunt pinned and still breathing below the busted Gatlin. Their knives came out, up, and then down over and over to finish that problem.

Two Harpers raced out of a hallway behind the parlor to escape deeper into the breached house. They ducked their heads and clutched their guns as they attempted to thread between the violence in the kitchen and the Finch-held front rooms.

Sabastian leveled and caved the head of the back fellow with a single shot. The boy slid on his face and joined those in the kitchen after all. Newt tracked the other with a swing of his rifle like a deer on the hoof. He fired and only missed clipping the corner of the wall under the stairs by no more width than a hair or maybe two. The bullet entered the Harper's ear and misshaped the skull of the opposite side without exiting. Blood belched out of the ear canal on entry and squirted out in a tight stream of pressure from the other. The boy spun in place and watered the floorboards from both ears like an automated sprinkler. His feet finally slipped out from under him, and he sprawled to his death. He surrendered his gun to the floor, and as his limbs came to rest, he carved an angel in his blood.

An old man burst from the opening in the back corner of the parlor. The distant nephews scattered away from the mangled corpse of the Harper aunt. Her black goggles lay askew on her puffy face. Her head looked deflated, her mouth open and dark.

The grandpa let loose with both barrels of his shotgun and blew apart what remained of the books on the shelf. He folded the gun open and shook out both spent shells before thumbing in two more red canisters full of shot. He locked it closed again and raised his eyes in time to see Sabastian shoot him square in the forehead.

The old man vanished backward into the hallway.

Newt stepped into the bloody hall between the stairs and kitchen. He swept his gun both directions, then turned on the cellar door. Gunfire continued through the house and in the kitchen with shrapnel flying all about. Newt spread his feet over the top of the bodies and kicked the door in. He fired twice to screams from below and took one step forward before the top of his head exploded across the ceiling. Newt's feet went out from under him, and his eyeballs rolled up from empty sockets into his open skull.

Sabastian's breath caught in his bone-dry throat as his second dead son fell onto the Harper boy's corpse.

The banister exploded and splintered next to Sabastian's head. He staggered away and slid down the foyer wall to his ass.

Susannah charged into the foyer with a bottle cocked above her head; the rag sopped in the clear liquid burned in the mouth of the bottle. Her arm came forward, but the bottle exploded, and two of her fingers twirled away as the bullet sailed outside. The liquid ignited and poured down Susannah's arm before engulfing her body. The Finch shooters perched by the door rolled away on the porch.

Sabastian stared as the body of flame collapsed to the foyer boards. Her impact sent liquid flame flowing up the stairs, along the floor toward Sabastian's boots, and up the paper of the wall next to his head. He finally breathed again, sucking in the poisoned fumes of the heat. His head swam and ached as he rolled away from the wash of burning death and scrambled like a frightened rodent into the parlor, barely staying ahead of the tide of fire.

Susannah's shrieks erupted from the fire with the sound of someone screaming on the inhale instead of the exhale.

Elizabeth charged through the threshold with another lit Molotov and planted her feet at the defiant edge of the pool of burning Susannah. This bottle flew, and the explosion at the top of the stairs came with more screams from above.

Kelly Harper tumbled head over ass down the steps as the fire climbed her body toward her head. She soared out over the last seven steps like a burning rocket and struck Elizabeth Finch square in the chest. Both women tumbled down the porch steps together, leaving puddles of fire in their path.

Black smoke filled the high ceilings and crept downward to Sabastian on the floor. He stood into the crawling darkness and leapt out through the parlor window, onto the porch with his eyes watering.

Elizabeth rolled away from the inferno of Kelly Harper's body. She dragged her arm and shoulder through the dirt toward the wall of the house to try to staunch the stubborn flames attached to her side. She sprawled against the base of the wall and tore the sizzling fabric away in melted strings of her own flesh. Blisters bubbled on Elizabeth's arm, shoulder, and neck between black scorches and raw pink. She turned her face to the sky and sucked air through clenched teeth.

Sabastian held his gun at the ready but watched Kelly burn. She screamed on the inhales and the exhales. It seemed such a shame to show her mercy by ending it all too soon.

Motion across the lawn drew his attention. Some barefoot boy Sabastian Finch did not recognize picked up the golden gun gifted from Castro himself off the hood it was left on. The boy ran around piles of broken glass as he fled up the street with his prize.

Sabastian leveled his gun and tracked the boy the way he had taught Newt to hunt. He blinked his wet eyes as smoke billowed out onto the porch behind him. The weapon clicked empty, and the boy ran away across the front of the church that was missing its steeple.

"I'll hang your balls from a stick when I track you down within whatever shack your parents fucked you into being."

Kelly's screams tapered off, and her chest heaved up a couple more times in her coffin of flame. Sabastian holstered the empty and drew a fresh weapon. He aimed and fired three times into the girl's chest before she could die on her own. It would have been a shame to have allowed her to die by any hand other than his own.

Now Carson … And Ratcliff … And every Harper, by blood or by marriage … ALL!

Finches clamored over porch railings from the side of the house. Howard, Spencer, Zachariah, and Mace's boy Cody ran past Sabastian without a word and jumped through the flow of smoke from the broken window.

Gunfire resumed inside the house instead of outside. He then heard a few stray shots from the street but did not look up immediately to see.

Sabastian opened and closed his fingers around the butt of his new pistol.

From inside, the strained voice of some man with an accent thick enough to be a gay man—or maybe from Mississippi—cried, "No, I'm a doctor, please. Don't do this."

Seven shots from multiple guns roared off at once, and the doctor begged no more.

The shooting continued outside too.

Cody shouted, "They're going down into the cellar. Come on."

Sabastian braced himself for the sound of more blasts of death from under the burning house, but then motion to his right drew his attention, and he forgot everything else.

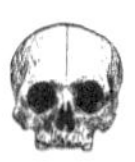

Gut shot.

Through the damn plaster without an aim. Brick, pipes, and solid plank lumber generations old should have stopped the lead in the dark recesses of the wall, but it came through in a hail of plaster and flowered paper to bite Ratcliff Harper in the flank.

The hot metal bored deep and sent waves of pain through the man's core. Ratcliff's shoulder shattered the glass cover over a photo of him with Carson and Norton as kids in a duck blind. Ratcliff's blood smeared over the yellowing paper, and the frame hung askew but stayed on the wall a while longer. Green bile oozed into the path of the bullet through Ratcliff's gut, and he folded to his knees on the floor.

Grandpa afforded him a look as he reloaded, but then returned fire outside.

Ratcliff tried to pull himself up the wall as he bled into the coat and down the leg of his seersucker, but he failed and remained knelt.

The front door burst in beyond the parlor. More plaster annihilated into dusty daylight around broken slats on the exterior wall. The ancient plank siding must have been chewed completely away from endless harassment.

"The house will never be livable again." A thick string of drool stretched from Ratcliff's lower lip to the floor. His dark hair hung in clumped strands over his forehead.

Grandpa did not offer him a look this time as he reloaded and stepped past the man of the house, now bleeding on the floor. Grandpa tracked Ratcliff's blood toward the parlor off the heel of one of his loafers.

Shouts and gunfire filled the kitchen. Tile spun through the air, and stray chips streaked through his blood on the hallway floor. His hand dropped from the wall to the floor. Ratcliff stared down the center hall between the parlor and kitchen in time to see a third cousin on his wife's side do a faceplant across the kitchen floor. Norton ran past the cellar door to take cover in the study, or one of the other backrooms maybe.

The bullet entered Norton's ear, and his skull came apart inside his head, twisting the boy's beautiful face into mongoloid distortions. Ratcliff saw his son's face only one more time clearly as Norton spun in place, bleeding from both ears. It was ugly and not how he wanted to remember the boy for however many minutes Ratcliff had left on this Earth. Norton went down, and his gun slid along the floor toward the study without him.

"All this for some shopkeeper's boy who wanted to bone a Harper instead of a Finch."

Grandpa fired both barrels into the parlor and reloaded. Should have taken one shot at a time. He barely closed the gun on a recharge before he took one to the forehead and fell to his back in the hallway, hugging his shotgun like a teddy bear.

One of the Finch boys stepped over Norton's still warm body and kicked open the cellar door.

All the children down there …

The Finch fired twice and took a step to finish everyone below the house. Ratcliff showed his teeth painted in a pink, half-bloodied film and raised his fist, almost surprised to see that he still clutched a weapon. He emptied it wild down the hall, but the noise of it blended with the endless ruckus in the kitchen.

The Finch boy's head tore off at the top, and he went down in a sandbag drop on top of Norton's body. Ratcliff's quivering lips twisted up into a smile.

His eyes slid half closed, and he slumped but did not reach the floor. Carson jerked his father to his feet and pulled him toward Grandpa's chair.

"I can't sit now, boy. Let me go."

Something exploded in the house behind them. Ratcliff felt the heat of it against his back and thought it might have been the kitchen.

Carson kicked Grandpa's chair over and shoved Ratcliff out the window. He twisted in the air and hit the ground in windless impact, staring into the sky in a tighter tunnel of dark pain than he had felt from the initial gut shot.

Carson stepped out into space and fell like a dark angel toward Ratcliff's skull. He landed next to the man and forced him to his feet again. Ratcliff moved his feet with no strength as Carson dragged his father across the side yard on his shoulder. He rolled Ratcliff over the side of a pickup and into the bed.

Ratcliff pulled himself up to sitting with a groan of dizzy pain.

He patted his pockets but found the rest of his holsters vacant from the empty weapons he had simply dropped in the heat of battle. He searched his bloody pockets, and his hands shook as he reloaded his gun with greasy bullets.

Carson started the truck, and they pulled away from the curb. The tires were flat, and the truck bounced as it ran over the lifeless bodies of Finches who had once hidden behind it.

Ratcliff cried out with each impact.

He heard shots close and looked up to see Mace Finch running up the middle of the road, firing on Ratcliff in the back of the stolen truck. They weren't driving fast enough in this battered machine. Ratcliff remembered playing poker with Mace when they were kids as he now took aim as an adult and shot at the man. Mace grabbed his shoulder and spun into the side of another truck before landing on his face in the street.

Ratcliff turned in time to see Sabastian Finch staring

at a burning body in the yard. Ratcliff emptied his gun at the porch but did not hit the bastard once. He dug for more blood-greased bullets as Sabastian turned and spotted them racing away on flattened tires.

Sabastian Finch raised his weapon and fired.

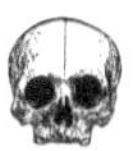

Three shots, and he missed with each one. Sabastian ran through the smoke to the end of the porch with another empty gun and watched that shitbird Carson drive his father toward the corner in one of the Finches' own trucks. No one manned the street to stop them or even see them. All the hell had moved in on the house as Ratcliff and one of his rodent offspring made off for any open sewer they could find.

Ratcliff lifted his shaky fist and extended his middle finger at Sabastian with a madman's grin pasted across his face.

Sabastian leapt over the railing and ran for the closest pickup. He rounded the grill and lifted his empty gun on a body hiding behind it. Mace rolled over, clutching his bloody shoulder, and said, "Don't shoot me again, you asshole."

Sabastian dragged his brother to his feet and opened the driver's door. He was already shoving Mace behind the wheel before he asked, "Can you drive?"

"If it's to rundown that rat bastard Harper, I'll steer with my dick if I have to."

Mace was already pulling away from the curb as Sabastian climbed in the passenger's door. He emptied his holsters of spent guns and laid them out on the rough fabric of the seat between himself and Mace.

Sabastian loaded the one in his hand first as they clattered by the back corner of the remains of the

Harper house. The garage was engulfed, with fire and smoke venting hard out every window. He looked over in time to see Boone shoot some woman through the back of her head where she lay face down next to a retaining wall.

Boone led the charge to the back door of the house and kicked his way in. Sabastian watched, just sure Boone's head would explode in his sight. His last child entered the back of the house still alive. Others poured in after him. Sabastian spotted Mr. Smith but not the noodle man's son. Smith ran inside as well with a gun in each fist.

The Harpers in a Finch pickup made a left at the stop sign. Sabastian pointed with the loaded gun. "There. Follow them."

"Yeah, I get what we're doing here. Just line up a shot as soon as I get you close."

Sabastian took up the next weapon off the seat and loaded it.

Mace made the turn at the corner. The pickup with Ratcliff in the back was a block and a half ahead.

"Go faster. We're not sneaking up on them, damn it."

"The tires are flat. I'm almost flooring it and fighting this bitch to stay straight on the pavement. We'll be running on the rims soon. Just hold on."

Sabastian gritted his teeth and continued to load his guns. "They turned at the courthouse. They're headed toward the park or the river. I bet they have a fishing boat down there. Let's move."

"Shut up." Mace blinked and gripped his bleeding shoulder with one shaky hand while driving with the bleeding arm.

The one-handed grip on the steering wheel didn't do much to keep the truck from fishtailing on the busted rubber of the tires and steel belts. Mace ran the one red light in town without pause. No one was driving through either way except the two bullet-riddled pickups. Two of the tires rolled off the rims in shreds, and the rims threw sparks in a constant spray behind the truck. The vehicle stayed straight but still felt like it spun its wheels on ice as Mace closed on the Harpers.

They drove past the empty parking lot of the Mason's Lodge with five or six car lengths between the trucks, and the Harpers turned away from the park to the river road and the docks.

They both hit the speed bumps, one after the other, and both trucks began to shimmy and rattle from whatever snapped loose underneath them.

Ratcliff's eyes went wide as he opened them and saw the Finches closing. Sabastian leaned out the window and aimed. Ratcliff let fly every round without the hassle of aim. Three of the shots broke through the windshield, and the rearview mirror fell into Mace's lap, causing him to wince and step on the accelerator. Ratcliff ducked to the side under the cover of the tailgate. That did not phase Sabastian, as he wasn't aiming at Ratcliff. A single shot punched through the back of Carson's head and sprayed the cracked windshield in red and thicker chunks of purple.

Carson's dead foot lifted off the gas, and the unmanned wheel lilted the pickup toward the water. With Mace's foot jammed on the gas, the sparking rims of the truck finally caught up and rammed the Harpers from behind, shattering two headlights on one vehicle and a taillight on the other. Sabastian's ear slammed into the window jamb where he leaned out, and he saw black stars. He dropped the nearly full pistol to the pavement, and the rest of the weapons flew off the seat, onto the floorboard.

The tail of the Harpers' truck spun through both lanes, losing the rest of the rubber off the rims. The spin would have gone fully around once—maybe twice—

from the collision as they hit the gravel on the shoulder of the road over the bank of the river, but gravity and dark water ended that spin nose first into the river.

Mace slammed the brakes as Sabastian leaned back and held his head. The wheels locked and skidded like knife blades over the street until they slammed into a telephone pole across from the river, coming to a stop in the ditch. Mace cracked the bridge of his nose on the steering wheel at the same moment Sabastian Finch opened his forehead on the dash.

The current caught the stolen truck and pulled it into the water. It finally finished its spin and came to rest against a shiny blue and white vessel tied to a private dock. The words The Great Adventure rocked above Harper as the bed filled with water and the truck settled into the mud beside the boat.

Sabastian grabbed up two guns from the floor and bailed out the passenger side. Mace rolled out of the open driver's door. He slid, bloody, down the side of the truck and sat in the mud and litter of the ditch with his head rested on the running board.

Sabastian leapt into the water and waded out to the truck. The bed was empty. He held both guns in one hand and felt in the water of the truck bed for a body. He tried to open the passenger door but couldn't budge it. The butt of one of his guns broke out the rest of the glass from the side window. Carson's lifeless body stewed in blood, filth, and river water. Sabastian smiled with blood running down his nose between his eyes but still wasn't satisfied.

He turned and waded upriver, under one dock after another. He looked into the shadows around each pylon. He swam under tethered boats and looked around the mud and the waving reeds.

He came up a fourth time after the last dock and saw the edge of the boardwalk ahead. Motion caught his attention, and he smiled again. He thumbed back the hammer and took aim, unsure if the wet bullets would still fire.

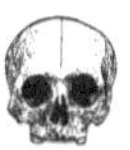

The shot did come, and it danced across the top of the water past Ratcliff's elbow as he entered the shadows under the boardwalk. He plunged forward into the darkness against the current and the dying weakness of the gut shot.

Couldn't be anything left to bleed out, could there? He was a walking corpse.

Another shot blasted green wood off the thick side of a pylon to Ratcliff's right.

He turned and slogged through the shallow with reeds wrapping his thighs. The plank wall under the fishery had a few sunken divots.

Ratcliff tried to dip his head in the water and submerge among the reeds. Too shallow. He couldn't go completely under even if he had breath left to hold.

He rose and turned back into one of the dark alcoves where the fishery's concrete foundation met the mud. He backed up until his back met the points of exposed nails.

Damn it. He wasn't deep enough.

Sabastian Finch's splashes echoed as he entered the cover of the boardwalk. His drawn, inhuman reflection wavered over the surface in front of Ratcliff's hiding spot.

Something gnawed at Ratcliff's stomach, and he bit down on his lip to stifle a groan.

"Ratcliff, you salty, childless bastard … Time to leave this world … Damn it …"

Ratcliff doubted Sabastian spoke to him directly.

Maybe didn't even realize he was speaking aloud at all.

He looked down and saw the ebony eyes of the serpent staring up at him. The black snake had its mouth folded open and its fangs embedded over the wound in his belly. Probably a moccasin. Maybe a cottonmouth. If there was one, there were many more. Maybe already attached to his legs or back. The venom and the blood loss had surely done him in.

If he thought letting Sabastian have his final revenge would bring his children back or end the Finches' rampage through distant relatives, he'd step right out and eat the bullet. He was dead anyway, but there was no stopping it.

Might as well make it as hard and unpleasant for the bastard as possible.

Ratcliff had no energy to pull the snake away, so he left it to do its killing business.

Sabastian passed in front of Ratcliff's spot. Ratcliff gritted his teeth and pressed back into the darkness, feeling the nails puncture his flesh and slide into his body. He felt certain at least one had found a kidney. The pain sharpened his vision instead of darkening it.

Sabastian turned and showed his teeth as well. "I hope they never find your body and it rots away under here forever."

Ratcliff launched himself off the nails and took Sabastian into his arms. Both guns in Finch's fists went off.

The guns went off again and again under the water before Sabastian lost his grip. Neither man knew how many times he was hit, but it was more than once each.

They surfaced once. One choked, "Mother ... fu ..." The other managed, "Die ..." Neither realized they had spoken. Black snakes latched to their cheeks, necks, and arms. One stabbed a fang into Sabastian's left eye where the color met the bloodshot white. The snake moved with the wild roll of the eye. The fang kept the lid from blinking closed. Another serpent latched over Ratcliff's lips, pinning them together in a bestial kiss.

They submerged again, locked onto one another tighter than the snakes. The men floated out under deeper water and held each other down. They each gripped the other in determination to see him drowned, and both ultimately succeeded long after their minds slipped too far away to register victory.

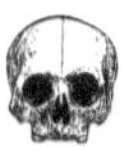

Mace Finch's eyes snapped open to the darkness of night. He moved and cried out against the fire in his clotted shoulder. He lumbered out of the ditch and away from the truck. He sneezed out thick green laced with black blood and groaned as the snot dangled from his chin.

Mace did not look at the river but limped up the street.

A blade of pink sliced the tops of the trees at the western horizon. It wasn't quite as late as Mace had thought.

He considered going back to get a gun from the truck but wiped his chin and decided against backtracking.

"Cody ..."

He limped along the river road toward the green ... yellow ... red ... green pattern of the one traffic signal ahead of him. Beyond that, dark smoke drifted up to blot out the first stars over the town.

"Cody?"

Mace was the head of the family now. He wasn't sure, but he suspected.

Jay Wilburn

Jay Wilburn was a prolific writer of horror, romance, YA, and science fiction, with hundreds of stories written and published. He won many awards during his astonishing and remarkable career. Along with his podcast, Matters of Faith, Jay was notable for his Patreon and Twitch feeds. While most writers would see others as competition, Jay saw them as friends, and he went out of his way to promote and encourage others. Jay passed away on October 18, 2022. He left an impact on the writing community that will never be forgotten.